# Carly the Zombie Slayer

michael paterson

Published by Michael Paterson, 2022.

CARLY THE ZOMBIE SLAYER

**First edition. July 31, 2022.**

Copyright © 2022 michael paterson.

ISBN: 979-8201520489

Written by michael paterson.

# Carly The Zombie Slayer

# Chapter One

I'm in a run-down, corner shop two days after my mother died. We're supposed to bury her tomorrow, and by We I mean Me. I need flowers to put on her coffin, and the only place in Prestonpans that has them at a reasonable price is this place called Everson's Grocery. The burial is at 9:00 a.m. If everything goes the way it usually does for me, I'll drink until I pass out, wake up hung-over at 8:50 a.m., shove on a tie, brush my teeth, and put the old woman in the ground with just minutes to spare. So yeah, there won't be time for flowers tomorrow. Besides, I don't want to linger in this town longer than I have to. We didn't talk much, Mother and I, she always liked my older brother Frank better; God knows why.

The rare occasions we did talk, I told her to give up those cigarettes, every time that I seen her. Two packs a day will kill you. No, she didn't die from lung cancer like I thought she would. She died in a car accident on her way to this very grocery store to, you guessed it, buy a pack of cigarettes. Go figure. Deer in the road, Officer Burnett said on the phone two days ago. Funniest thing I'd ever seen. Already dead, but not from a car. Something had eaten it, the deer. A bear, maybe. Thing is, we don't get bears around here...ever. Oh well, sorry about your mother, Carly. She was a...pleasant woman. A pleasant woman who suffered an unpleasant death.

She's gone and I'm still here. I was going to call her in a couple weeks on her birthday. I was going to apologize for being a shitty daughter, make amends. Now she's dead. Life is cruel that way, I guess, and it only seems to get worse because whatever was eating the deer found my mom's totaled car and thought she must've looked tastier. It's safe to say we'll be having a closed coffin memorial service. The bright white lights of Everson's Grocery almost blind me. I pass the front counter where the cartons of cigarettes and rolls of scratch-offs sit on display like diamonds for the white trash who shop here, keeping my head and eyes straight in front.

Laser focus. One goal in mind, Roses, red roses, In and out. No small talk, no fake condolences. Nothing. I see the blonde behind the glass out of the corner of my eye as she gives me the look, the look they give outsiders in Prestonpans, home of the Woodchucks. "Carly?" she says. "Carly Glass, is that you?" I ignore her, keep walking. If I stop, I'm afraid of who will be the owner of that voice. She might be Darla Sterling, the bleach-blonde, head cheerleader who turned me down for the Homecoming Dance freshman year by way of composing an elaborate, new fight song that consisted of "F-U-C-K Y-O-U, B-I-T-C-H!" and "Hell no, I won't go!" Clever, I know.

Or she might be Lexi George who once spread a rumor of me eating out of garbage cans when I was a junior, a rumor that caught like wildfire. Maybe Eden Fenway, my personal favorite, whom I vomited on at a bonfire senior party. Two plates of spaghetti and meatballs plus vodka are never a winning combination. I was pulling out whole noodles from my mouth like a clown pulls out those colorful handkerchiefs. It was never-ending, man. See, there are too many risks coming back to the place where you grew up, especially a small town where everyone knows everything about each other.

What you had for dinner. Who gave you your first kiss in the back seat of your mother's car. When you have your morning bowel movement. Who's cheating on each other. I knew coming in here would be like walking through a minefield while blindfolded. Small towns have their own gravitational pull about them. It's charming. It's safe. It's warm. People can leave, go off to college, maybe work a big-city job, but they always come back. Ten years after high school, and I didn't. That's pretty good, a new Prestonpans record, perhaps. Two Towns separate me from this godforsaken place, and sometimes I don't even think that's enough.

I smell fresh roast beef as I silently curse my mom for dying. I'm not sad, not as sad as I should be, I suppose. Maybe it'll hit me later when I'm half a bottle in and reruns of The Golden Girls play on the fuzzy television the Prestonpans Motel has in room 101. That was her favorite show. I don't know why I remember this or why it comes to me now. I think if it happens, I'll just click off the TV. Problem solved. But I probably won't. The butcher with his blood-stained apron and scraggly beard, likely in violation of some or all health codes, gives me the same look as the blonde. I'm not quick enough to play it cool, so I nod my head.

His lips part, my name already on the tip of his tongue, and I duck into the candy aisle. Chocolate wall-to-wall, floor-to-ceiling. Friggin minefield, I tell you. And it just gets worse. The man standing in the aisle beyond the chocolate about twenty feet away from me is Freddy Huber, Former, star quarterback of the fierce Woodchucks, Same graduating class as me. My mortal enemy, even if he doesn't know it. I don't know how many wedgies I took from this guy, how many gameboys that he knocked out of my hand in primary school, how much milk he poured on my head or pudding down my back.

Too, many to count. Then in high school it got worse. Broken noses, sucker punches, spitballs in the back of the head, in Mr. Berry's class. A constant barrage of gay jokes. Mother jokes, runaway dad jokes these always hurt worse than his fists. I hate him and myself at the same time. Because seeing this guy makes me shudder. I'm sweating despite the frozen food being on the other side of the chocolate shelves. He's got a couple bottles of cold medicine in hand. DayQuil and NyQuil in the throes of a scorching Scottish summer, but I'm not surprised. It seems like everyone is sneezing, coughing, and shuffling around like they're on the edge of death since I've gotten here.

Flu season has come early. I back away toward the smell of roast beef, clenching my ass as phantom hands pull at my underwear, threatening another atomic wedgie. "Carly?" Freddy says. Fuck. Too late. I could run, but running only makes it worse. I know from experience...a lot of experience. In three quick strides he's on me, a large mitt smacking my shoulder hard. "Holy shit! It is you! I thought you died or something. Rumor around town was you killed yourself.

I felt so bad. All those years of torment, my ex-wife said I probably had a hand in it." He snorts, very mucus-y. "But she's a bitch." He's smiling as he says all of this as if me dying is the joke of the century. "Nope, still here," I say, and sometimes I think that's both a blessing and a curse. Many vodka bottles have been drained in an attempt to forget all about Freddy Huber's torment. Freddy hasn't lost his quarterback stature. Broad shoulders. Strong jaw. Thick arms. Six feet tall. But now he has a beer belly, and the full head of blonde hair is thinning as we speak.

I think about what he'll look like in another ten years and I start to smile. "Well, that's good, Really good." "Yeah, I guess it is." "What you doin' nowadays? Figured you'd be like a math magician or something," Freddy says. "I...work from home." "Yeah, doin' what?" "I'm a writer." Laughter erupts from Freddy, drowning out the slow jazz playing over the loudspeakers. He drops his hand basket. The purple bottle of NyQuil rolls a few feet away. "A writer? Like for the newspaper?" "Books, mostly. Short stories here and there. Hardly any money in those." When I start talking about writing, it's hard to stop. Even to this big buffoon. "So you must be rich as hell, huh?" I shrug. No, not rich at all. "What'd you clear last year? Couple million?" He smiles, but his eyes have lost all sense of geniality. "I don't know...around seventy-five." "Whoo, boy! Seventy-five thousand just from sitting on your ass and makin' shit up?" I notice his smile disappears.

His face darkens like we're back in the boy's locker room after gym class, just me and him and a wet towel. "Know what I made last year?" he asks, then turns his head to cough. The lights overhead hit his skin at just the right angle and I begin to realize how sick this guy is. Pasty. Yellow. Sweaty. I shake my head. I don't know what he made last year, but I could probably guess. He hasn't left town so he has to work at the mill on Lite Street or at the government testing facility just outside the city lines. Since Freddy had me do his homework for a large portion of high school, I think it's safe to say this asshole isn't working a government job.

Hell, he might still be delivering pizzas. "I made twenty-five breaking my back at the fuckin steel mill." He jabs a finger at me. Vaguely, behind him, I see a few people watching our friendly, little exchange. "Can you believe that shit? I work sixty hours a week, sweating my balls off, and Carly Glass is sitting in an air conditioned office, letting all her dumbass ideas come to life on a computer screen, making more than me. What a crock." He tries to raise his voice but can't.

All that comes out is a sputtering wheeze, like a dying engine. "Well, I probably shouldn't say I'm on track to make double that this year." I speak with a smile on my face. It feels good to watch his features melt into something akin to a rage soup. But the fist that comes whistling through the air doesn't. It clobbers me at what seems like a million miles per hour. I feel something crack. My vision fuzzes like a TV that lost its signal. For a moment, the punch knocks me back to the halls of Prestonpans High ten years ago, hearing the laughter of all Freddy's football goons and tasting my own blood.

# Chapter Two

Freddy hasn't lost any of his strength despite whatever bug he has. I'm never that lucky. My head spins, eye already swelling shut. He yells something at me, but I can't understand it. My ears are ringing. Other people in the store must've gathered around because I hear them clamoring. A sea, of incoherent babbles. I push myself up, feeling a drop of blood or maybe a tear rolling down my cheek. My hand comes up to feel the spot that got rocked, and I wince. "see if you can write a fuckin book with broken fingers," Freddy shouts. I'm dimly aware of him advancing on me. He's exactly the type of guy who'll kick you while you're down old habits die hard, I guess so I try to pull myself up, using the shelf of cold medicines and cough drops as hand rungs.

It's not as successful as I need it to be. Freddy grabs me, pulls all one-hundred and fifty pounds of my body weight off the floor as if I weigh less than half of that. "Stop it!" I hear someone shout. "Freddy Huber, you get the hell outta my store or I'm callin the police." Then I hear a loud click-click. Freddy turns his head around, giving me a chance to retaliate, but I can't. I don't even think I could stand on my own two feet without help, let alone swing a fist. Doesn't matter anyway because Freddy drops me.

He puts his hands to his mouth as he stifles a cough, then they go above his head. "Mr. Everson, always a pleasure," he says through a thick veil of mucus. "Cut it, Huber," Mr. Everson says. I can't see the man, but I think: Everson's still alive? The Everson as in Everson's Grocery? God, he must be ninety-years-old by now. "Hey, I'm a paying customer." "Not no more, Huber. Get the hell outta here. We don't need this type of crap." "But Glass started it." "Somehow, I highly doubt that. Get out of the store. Next time you want groceries or booze, you can go to North Berwick. Make a scene there, let them deal with you." Freddy slowly backs up, his hands still raised. I shuffle out of his way, my eye almost swollen shut, head still thrumming with fear and a little bit of rage. "All right, all right, Mr. Everson."

Then he looks down at me with a grin, "This ain't over, Shakespeare." "Out...now!" Everson says. I realize the old man holds a shotgun and he points it higher, aiming at Freddy's head. I know Everson won't shoot, but if he does, I'm in the blast radius. Thankfully, Freddy shuffles out, laughing and saying, "Wait'll my dad hears about this!" He points at me. "Next time I see you, Glass, I'm gonna eat you alive!" "Not if I gouge out your eyes, you sorry asshole!" I make a move, but Everson blocks me, still on my hands and knees.

To the spectators, it's probably pathetic, but I like to think it's valiant. Heroic, maybe. "Not worth it. Let him go," Everson says. I know he's right, but I'm done getting bullied. It's not why I came back to this shithole town. The bells over the front door jingle, signaling his departure and believe me, you can hear it all the way from the front of the store, it's that quiet in here. Mr. Everson hands a young bag-boy his weapon and walks over to where I try to pull myself up. "You good, son?" "Yeah," I say. My one good eye is open as wide as it can be. Everson sees it and smiles. "Don't worry, it ain't loaded. All for show. Ninnies like Huber always fall for the empty shotgun."

Then he pauses and extends a gnarled hand out to help me up. "Listen, you can come in the back and we'll get that blood cleaned up. Officer's on his way, too, in case you wanna file a report." I shake my head. "No, I'm good. Just needed to get some roses." "No, no, that's a nasty cut, son. Needs some peroxide on it. You don't have to file a report but at least let me fix you up." Then after a moment's hesitation, he says, "Say, don't I know you?" I rub at the gash under my eye. It's slick with blood now. "Yeah, yeah, I know you," Everson says. "You're that kid who wound up writing those scary books.

I read the one about those monsters in that small, mountain town and the one with them flesh-eating zombies. Boy, I love a good zombie story." I nod, smiling. Everson is the last reader I'd expect to have, and probably the only person who loved the zombie book. Not my finest hour, I'll admit. "Ain't your momma Nadine?" I nod. "Rest her soul. Terrible thing that happened to her." He turns, shaking his head and motioning to me. "Come on back, dear." Everyone watches us, their eyes lighting up with realization. Yeah, I'm that kid who was utterly forgettable in high school, who got out and made something of herself. To them, I'm like a God. I don't have stress wrinkles from barely making the rent each month.

My back isn't stooped from manual labor. I don't have the same pair of shoes on that I had on ten years ago. I'm clean, sober, and dare I say...happy? It's a sad realization for us both, I'm sure. And I can't say no to Everson. So I nod and he puts his arm through mine as if to look like he's helping me, but he's so old that I end up helping him.

# Chapter Three

The break room isn't much, and though the store part has recently been renovated to look like it just entered the mid-nineties, the back looks more like the seventies. The floor is checkered black and white, but the white is more of a dingy color, like an old cheese, maybe even a corpse. There's a microwave on the counter with dried remnants of a nuked burrito leaking from between the closed door. I know it's a burrito because I smell the beans and cheese. The clock on the wall is shaped like a cat and each time a second goes by the cat's tail swishes back and forth. I think the eyes are supposed to move, but they don't. Instead, they stare emptily into the far corner of the break room. "Have a seat," Everson says. He goes to a cabinet and sorts through old boxes of instant coffee. Behind a Kenco container, he pulls free a black bottle of peroxide. I don't know why he keeps the peroxide with the coffee, but I don't get a lot of things in Prestonpans and I lived there for eighteen years. Besides, peroxide is needed, if not for the cuts then for the germs of whatever bug Freddy's carrying. I really don't feel like getting my ass kicked and catching the flu.

Everson dabs it onto a cotton ball, then hands it to me. I press the cold fuzz to my face. It stings. "That Huber kid has always been a bully," he says. "Just like his daddy." "I don't know his dad, but I believe it," I say. "You'd think with a big-wig job like the one his dad got, he would've turned out better." I nod, vaguely registering an image of Freddy Huber's father at his big-wig job. I see him behind a desk, suit and tie, steaming cup of coffee in front of him. He yells for his secretary to pick up his dry cleaning. It's funny because I would've pictured his dad to be gone like everyone else's around here seems to be, mine included.

And seeing how Freddy wound up at the steel mill, I'm even more surprised that his dad has a so-called big-wig job. "Where's his dad work?" I ask. "Up at the Redburn, Research Facility." I nod. Yep, like I said before, here in Prestonpans, you really only have two choices: work at the mill or some other dead-end minimum wage job, or go to college and get a job at the Research Facility. There is a third option, too. It's kill yourself, but something tells me you'll just end up right back in Prestonpans. Like I have. "Too bad the shotgun wasn't loaded," Everson says, grumbling. "Back when I was his age, you do something like that and you're spending the night in the cells. But the police will let him off the hook. He's too soft." "No big deal," I say, getting up. "Thanks for the peroxide." "Where ya going, dear? I don't think you're fit to drive yet." "I can't stay," I say. "I've got a funeral to co-ordinate. My friend is gonna be wondering where I'm at.

You know how women are." Everson snorts, his wrinkled cheeks wrinkling up even more to smile. "Don't I just," he says. The door to the break room opens and in walks Officer Burnett. He's been in the force since long before I was born, but he doesn't look as ancient and decrepit as Mr. Everson. Somehow, he looks only a few years older than me, but he has to be pushing fifty or sixty. He's a big man, too, the type of guy you'd expect to be wheeling around town in an SUV that says PRESTONPANS POLICE DEPT stenciled on the side. I hear the floor creak beneath his weight. A glint of dark metal catches my eye. Burnett carries around a big-ass gun on his hip, like an Old West Marshall. I don't know if it's a standard weapon or if he's added a few cosmetic modifications to it. He doesn't need the weapon, either.

The worst that happens in this town is someone gets too drunk and pisses in the middle of the high Street. A bar fight here or there. Petty theft. Someone gets punched in the face. Nothing crazy. Nothing like the Old West, many years ago. The next thing that catches my eye is the blood on the outside of his Carlyet. There's a few drops, not a lot but enough to make me think, What the hell? Everson notices it, too. I can tell by the way he scrunches up his face. "Burnett, what's with the blood? Halloween ain't for another three months."

Burnett looks down and scoffs. "Damn it," he says. His voice is high and somewhat feminine. Another reason why I think he likes to carry around that big gun, compensation. He grabs a roll of paper towels, tears off a wad, and starts wiping at the blood. It doesn't do much good, only fades the stains slightly. "You been killin bad guys again?" Everson says, chuckling. "No, it was Dan out on the coast road. One of his cows." "One of his cows?" Everson repeats. I'm sitting in the old chair with plastic covering on its back, trying to think of a way out of here where both men won't notice me leaving. "Yeah, that's what I said, one of his cows. Something got into his pasture. Tore it right up into pieces. And you know Dan, he's almost as old as you, ya old geezer.

I had to help him move the damn thing out of the field before the other cows got curious." He shakes his head, "Shit, they don't pay me enough for this." "It's that damn research center out there," Everson says. "Ever since that fire, things just ain't been the same." I don't keep up with Prestonpans current events, that much is true, but a fire? At, Red-burn? Surely, I would've heard about a fire. Unless...unless they didn't want anyone to hear about it. This oddly seems like one of my own books, shady government research facility, cows being eaten by some mysterious monster. A light goes off in my head. Werewolf, that's what it is. It's got to be.

I smile and roll my eyes, hoping neither Burnett or Everson see me. This is the way I get when I'm deep into a new story. I link every small thing to whatever I'm working on, try to prove to myself that I'm going crazy. You should've seen me with the Ebola outbreak a couple of years ago. I was working on the zombie novel then. Diane, my best friend almost kicked me out of the apartment. So that's all this is, coincidence and me going crazy. "Oh, please, Bill, they got it under control up there," Burnett says, waving a hand. He looks at me, a wry smile on his face. "Besides, right now we have more pressing matters to attend to, right, Glass? I hear you're already getting into trouble.

You only been here a day...should I be worried? Am I gonna have to cuff you like I did when you was in middle school?" Everson bursts out laughing. "I 'member that one." Heat rises to my cheeks. I really shouldn't have come back to this town. Or I at least should've driven the extra few miles and picked up some flowers in Edinburgh, hell, even North Berwick. "Yeah, yeah, real funny," I say. "What'd ya steal? I can't remember," Burnett says. "Wasn't it toothpaste or something?" "Reese's Peanut Butter Cups," I say. "The toothpaste I got away with." "Still don't understand it, kid.

You was smarter than that. Look at you now, making a living by typing all fancy like. Oh, shoot, that's a good story to tell to my drinking buddies: 'You know that famous writer, the one who writes about ghosts and goblins and ghouls? Carly Glass is her name, well I arrested her in eighth grade. Caught her stealing candy and toothpastes down at Everson's. Little girl damn near pissed her pants when I cuffed her!'" Burnett slaps the counter, laughing. Everson laughs with him, but his laughs are more like croaks.

I wouldn't be surprised if dust starts pouring out of the old man's mouth. "Real funny," I say again. "Why'd you do it?" Everson says. "I mean I forgive ya, but why? Your mama wasn't poor." "Just wanted to fit in, I guess," I say. It's not as hard to talk about it now than it was then, and my explanation is partially true. I did want to fit in. When all the kids in my grade were out shooting deer with their grand-dads, stealing candy bars from Everson's, and sticking firecrackers up bull-frogs's asses, I was back at home reading stories about evil wizards and Hobbits, and watching movies about spaceships. But another reason I did it was because I wanted to see if I could get away with it. I didn't, obviously. "Let me see that shiner," Burnett says.

I pull away the cotton pad. It sticks as I do it, and the pain is almost unbearable, but I can't show it in front of these two. Burnett's eyes go big. "Damn, girl, Huber really do that to you?" "Yeah," I say. "Damn right he did. That man ain't nothing but a menace," Everson says. "Wouldn't be the first time I've seen the bastard pick a fight. Remember last year's July 4th parade when he got in the scuffle with Franky Williams?" Burnett nods. "Unfortunately I do. Sometimes I'll walk down the high street and still think I see some of Frankie's teeth on the sidewalk." "It's no big deal, really," I say, interrupting their trip down memory lane. "Freddy's a bully, always has been.

# Chapter Four

He looked like he was coming down with a nasty cold, too. Maybe that'll be punishment enough." "Flu season gets longer and longer every year," Burnett says. "Been going around something vicious this spring, all over town. Dan was coughing his damned head off. First these coyotes, or bears or whatever, eating all the wildlife and farm animals, and now the summer flu. What's next, we have to cancel the Fourth of July festival?" Everson gasps, real concern written on his face. The Fourth of July is a big deal around here. Burnett laughs. "Not a chance," he says, then turns back to me and shrugs. "I'm telling ya," Everson says, "ever since that fire, things ain't been the same. I drive by it sometimes and it looks about as haunted as that house up on Seton Hill."

Ah, the Seton Hill haunted house, the basis of the first novel I sold. One time Frank made me go up to the front door when I was nine despite my constant protests. I couldn't say no to my older brother. I had to prove I was as brave as he was. When we got to the front porch, he bolted. I remember hearing noises in there, screams and the sounds of axes coming down on people's heads. All just my imagination, no doubt, but I almost couldn't run away. Later that night, I lost about twenty pounds of sweat and didn't sleep right for a month. Burnett rolls his eyes. "Why don't you ask Freddy's dad?" "Haven't seen him.

Good riddance," Everson says. His face looks as if he'd just swallowed something bitter. I smile, but that's as far as I can contribute to this conversation. It's been too long. I'm no longer in "the loop", if you can call the ever-turning wheels of the gossip train "the loop." "Well, if you don't want to file nothing against Freddy," Burnett says, "it'll save me a helluva lot of paperwork." "No, don't worry about it. I'll heal." "Sounds good, kid," Burnett says, sticking a hand out at me. "Then we're good here? I can leave?" I ask, accepting his handshake. Everson looks to the Officer. "Yeah, I guess so," Burnett says. I get up.

The chair scrapes the molded linoleum beneath me, and I head for the door. "Wait, Glass. One more thing," the Officer says. I'm halfway into the dark hallway. I can see the light at the end of the tunnel. The light of the grocery store which leads to the parking lot and my freedom. "I had to call your brother," Burnett says. "He's coming back for the funeral." It's so quiet after Burnett tells me this, I think they might be able to hear my knuckles grinding together as I squeeze my hands into fists. "I had to, Carly. She loved him as much as she loved anything, and she's his mother, too." "Thanks, Officer," I say as I walk out into the darkness. I try not to sound like an asshole. The door latches behind me. All that's going through my head is that I really shouldn't have come back home.

Prestonpans Motel is a seedy place on the corner of Ayres Wynd and Cranberry Avenue. Cranberry is that street my mother told me to stay away from whenever I rode my bike around town with my brother, a long stretch of blacktop that leads in and out of town. There's a place that was once a church across the way. Empty black squares have long since replaced the glass. The door, a towering oak, has been battered and rammed and is now almost always open. It's a hangout for the homeless and the drug addicts. Lots of lorries drive through. Some of these drivers peddle meth and heroine.

Not much the small police force can really do about it, either. Plus, I think Officer Burnett takes a cut. No way he, could afford a watch like the one he had on, back at Everson's. I park my car in the empty space. I'm sitting between two faded lines on the blacktop that might've once been yellow. We are in room 101, the farthest from the office. It may be ten years since I've been back in Prestonpans, but I remember the stories about the motel. Once upon a time, there was talk of expansion, even a second floor, hence the room 101. That never happened because the funding fell through. Poor, creepy Mark Hutchins, the guy who owns it. He's owned it as long as I can remember.

Rumors say he likes to blast porn in the dead of night. Some others say they've caught him looking in at them through a hole in the wall. Others talk of cameras he's placed in hiding spots in every room. Really, I doubt it. This place doesn't make enough money for him to afford spy gadgets. But when I open up the door, I can't help but notice all the sheets I draped over various places in the room: microwave, old TV, the mirrors. Diane is sitting in a plush chair with puke-green upholstery. She's reading a book, something even I wouldn't read and damn sure would never write about, and I've written a zombie novel for God's sake; it almost doesn't get any lower than that. Diane's book is a love story with a bare-chested man on the cover. You know, the kind that has every woman's wet dream within the confines of its three hundred poorly written pages.

Happily ever after and all that. Lovey dovey...vomit. Her eyes barely flicker over the top of the paperback as I walk in. "When you gonna read one of mine?" I ask. "When you stop killing characters and start making them fall in love," she says. Diane is the most beautiful thing in this room by a mile, hell, she might even be the most beautiful thing in this town. She puts the book down on her lap, still open. When she looks at my face, really looks at my face, the book comes tumbling down onto the shag carpet. "Oh, Carly, what happened?" Before I know it, her hand is cupping my chin, pulling me closer. I wince. Freddy's haymaker did more than just split open my cheek and bottom lip; it made my whole damn face tender. "Just ran into an old friend," I say. "Carly," she says in that way that really means cut the bullshit. "An old high school bully," I say, smiling. "Did you call the cops?" "Officer came, nothing happened." "My God," she says. "He should be in jail." I grab her around the waist, pull her closer. "No, he's just some bitter wash-up.

I may have mentioned how much I was on track to make this year with the book sales. So I'm no angel, either." Besides, it's not like I'm making millions. Any old schmuck can write about ghosts and zombies. Instead of gloating, I should've given him words of encouragement. Hindsight is 20/20, isn't it? Diane and I hug, and for a moment, the pain in my face subsides. "I'm just glad you're okay," she says when we part. I sit on the side of the bed and start taking off my shoes. The mattress damn near sinks to the floor with my weight, and I don't weigh much. "That's not even the worst of it," I say. "I'd rather get punched in the face again by that asshole than find out what the Officer told me." "What? What did he tell you?" Diane asks. She crawls up next to me, drapes her arms around my shoulder. I can feel her hot breath on my earlobe. It gets the blood pumping in all the right places, but I choose to ignore it. "He told me my brother is coming to the funeral. Can you believe that?" "You said he wouldn't show. You said there was a ninety-five percent chance he wouldn't show." "Well ninety-five ain't a hundred," I say.

"So what's the plan?" she asks as she slowly kisses me on the neck."We bury my mom, then we get the hell out of here before Frank can start harassing me about the 'good ol' days.'" "Maybe that's not a bad thing, Carly. You don't have anyone left." "I got you," I say. She smiles. "Not what I meant. Maybe we should stay... You can't go living your life like a hermit. This is your hometown. Your mom just passed and now your brother is coming back. Maybe you should reconcile. I mean, what if he dies tomorrow?" Good riddance, I almost say, sounding like Mr. Everson in my head. "You don't want to live with that, do you?" I don't answer, and she knows I don't because she's right.

God, I hate it when she's right. She nibbles my ear, whispering, "Come on, Carly, it'll be good for you to have some time off. Me, too. I have three weeks of paid holidays saved up. We can stay five more days, and you can show me around a little more. I'd love to see where my future partner grew up." I feel her lips curl up into a smile, pressing against my neck. A hand slips around my waist, rubs up my inner thigh. When she gets like this, she's The Godfather, not the sexiest comparison, I know, but her offers, I can't refuse. "Okay," I say, "Five more days. That's all. You'll get the Carly Glass Grand Tour. Prepare yourself." She squeezes me and lets out a satisfied moan. How the hell can I say no to her? To this?

# Chapter Five

After we talk for awhile, Diane's head lays on my chest. I hear her breathing deepen. She's falling asleep and I'm soon to follow if I don't get out from under these sheets. They're damp with sweat, faintly smelling like mothballs, an odd combination that's surprisingly pleasant to the senses. But my laptop sits in a case on the desk across the room, mocking me. I need to get some work done.

The words won't write themselves as much as I wish that were the case sometimes. Diane rolls over off of me to lie on her side. "Good night," she says, turning to face me, a faint smile on her lips. "That was good, but we're supposed to save it until our wedding night." "You said the same thing yesterday morning," I say. It's how this whole engagement has gone. I give her a wink, and kiss her on the cheek. "Good night." "Better get to bed pretty soon. You'll have to be up early for the..." She trails off. "Don't remind me."

Diane pulls the sheets up around her shoulders, covering her milky, white skin. Bedtime for her usually means work time for me. She's the type of person who'll be in bed by nine, and I'll be up until four in the morning, sometimes later. And sometimes I'm still up when she rolls out of bed for work at 7:00 a.m. If we were back at our apartment in Carlisle, I'd make her coffee and some pancakes, but the best I can do here is vending machine snack foods and Coca-Cola.

I decide to pump out some words. It's not easygoing, my mind runs through all the bullshit I've been through in the last few days, but somehow I write a chapter in the werewolf book I've been working on, loosely inspired by what Burnett and Everson told me about the Leering Research Facility. The clock magically moves at the speed of light. Before I know it, two hours roll by. I get up to stretch. It's stuffy in the motel room, the smell of sex now gone. I need fresh air so I open the door to step out. Moonlight bathes me in a glorious white, you don't get this type of thing in the city where electricity chokes out Mother

Nature. I have no shirt on, only wearing my gym shorts and a beaten pair of slippers. It doesn't matter because there's no one in the motel parking lot. No cars roll down the street. Far up the walkway I see the light from Mark Hutchins's TV set. Faintly, the voices carry through the door.

I walk up about halfway where a couple of vending machines sit against the brick wall between the rooms. The colors of the Coca-Cola machine are faded, almost acid-washed. Caffeine. I'll need it if I'm going to bust out another chapter tonight. Johnny, this new editor at my publisher, is a regular Nazi when it comes to deadlines, dead mother or not. There are two quid in twenty pence's in my short's pockets. I have a membership to Gold's Gym back in England, but I don't do much working out. Usually, I just walk on the treadmill while Diane does her spin class. The change is for snacks in case she keeps me waiting too long. I know it's a bad habit, but remember I'm a writer, not some world class athlete.

Not surprisingly, a can of coke is only seventy pence around here. So I buy two and start looking at the one next to it. It houses an array of snack foods: Twinkies, Hostess Cupcakes, Cinnamon Rolls, Snickers, Reese's. I try not to think about how old they might be when I pop in seventy-five more pence. A Reese's slowly starts to uncurl from the wire which holds it in place. My mouth salivates at the phantom taste of sugar and salt, milk chocolate and peanut butter. Then it stops, the package dangling on the edge. "You gotta be kidding me," I say, rubbing my head.

This place just gets worse and worse. I look around the lot again. All the rooms are dark, I don't think there's any other guests but Diane and me. Black windows, closed drapes, no cars. My mind is made up. I give the machine a shove. The glass vibrates, but other than that, nothing happens. No Reese's. I grab hold with two hands, start rocking the damn machine back and forth. Again, nothing. "Damn," I say under my breath. I could try for another snack, but all I got is fifty pence, and the damn machine will probably eat that too, Maybe Diane will want a Coke in the morning, Screw that, I'm cheap.

I may be looking to double my income this year with book sales, but that doesn't mean money grows on trees. So I walk up toward the motel office where I hear studio laughter leaking from beneath the door (not porn), I don't bother knocking and walk right in. Mark is watching an old re-run of Happy Days. The television plays in the corner and looks ancient. He doesn't even notice me at first, so I clear my throat. Like the vending machine, no response. I do it louder this time. He swivels around, his eyes wide, looking like he just got caught yanking one out at church.

Mark leans forward and turns the volume knob all the way down. "Carly, how ya doing?" he says in a southern drawl that's not native to Prestonpans. "The room all good for ya? That pretty fiancé happy?" He says the last part with a wink, causing a couple droplets of sweat to roll down from his hairline. I skip the small talk, get right to the point. Truth is, this bastard creeps me out, even without the rumors of spying on the guests. "Vending machine ate my money.

I wanted a Reese's." "Oh, hell, I've been meaning to fix that. Called the vending machine company 'about six months ago and they ain't never showed up. Go figure. 'Round here we gotta do things ourselves, but you know that, don't ya, lil Carlyy?" He chuckles. "Yep," I say, knowing Mark will never get around to fixing the machine and neither will the company who owns it, either. He kind of stares blankly at me for a moment, as if he's mentally, checked out.

I attribute it to either slight retardation or just way too much booze. It's probably the latter, but I've never been able to rule out the former. Then he shakes his head. "Alright I'll see what I can do." Mark gets up. He's a thin man, maybe too thin. He looks like he already has one foot in the grave. "I'll be right back," he says, leaving the room. Like coming back home, I realize trying to get my measly seventy-five pence was probably a mistake.

I look around, and the office is smaller than the motel rooms and somehow looks even more trashed. Diane might call it chic or some other weird fashion term. There's wood paneling on the walls. The desk is made out of solid oak, polished. On the floor is a rug of psychedelic colors: red and blue and green and yellow. An empty water cooler hums in the background. I catch a faint whiff of mold and smoke, despite there being a sign above a notice board behind the counter reading: NO SMOKING.

The notice board is filled with flyers. Some look as old as the building, the corners of the pages curled up and discolored. Others look newer, one, in particular, catches my eye. It's next to another newer one that says:

COME DOWN TO THE TOWN SQUARE FOR OUR 68TH ANNUAL FIREWORK FESTIVAL. PARADE! FOOD! BOOZE! GAMES! FUN! FUN! 7-12, YOU CAN PARK AT JOE'S. FISH BAR

A few shakily drawn firework displays are above the words. But the flyer that caught my eye shows a picture of a man I faintly recognize. This one is done up more professionally. The words read,

MUSCULAR HEAVEN WITH KEVIN. TRAIN HARD. GET RIPPED. CALL PRESTONPANS REC- CENTER FOR AVAILABLE TIMES. OPEN SEVEN DAYS A WEEK.

I smile at the picture. It looks a lot like Kevin Jenkins, one of the few friends I had in high school. He was just as nerdy and pathetic as I was, but when we went off to college we lost touch. He probably weighed about 130, tall as hell. A strong wind would've blown him out of town, but now, unless it's Photoshopped, he looks more Goliath than David. I walk behind the desk and grip a tab with the name (that does, in fact, say Kevin Jenkins) and number on the flyer and rip it off.

Kill two birds with one stone here, I think. Learn some work-out techniques and catch up with an old friend. As long as I'm stuck in town I might as well, right? Mark shuffles in with a key ring. He stops and gives me a crooked gaze. "Whatcha doin' behind my desk?" "Flyers," I say. "Aw, yeah. You gonna stick around for the fireworks?" I wish I could say no, but the truth is, I am. "Maybe," I say. "Good, good," Mark says. "Now let's go get you your Reese's." He walks out of the office, with me trailing behind him. I still have the paper in my hand with Kevin's name on it. I'll call him in the morning after the funeral. For now, I look forward to a chocolate and peanut butter cup of deliciousness.

lot about a five minute walk from the town square. I wear black dress pants, a white undershirt, and a black suit jacket — no tie. I have a pair of sunglasses over my eyes despite it not being too sunny yet. The time is 9:13 a.m. The date is July 2nd. It is Friday. We didn't have calling hours for my mother yesterday. She didn't want them and rightfully so. She wasn't well-liked in the community if I'm being totally honest. She was just kind of there. So far, it's just me, Diane, the priest who I don't recognize and a couple of meaty employees who helped carry the coffin. At least they're dressed nicely. The priest coughs into his arm a couple of times, then pulls a handkerchief free from his pocket. I look straight at him as a glob of blood hanging on his lip is wiped away.

It's gross, but as of right now, I am numb. "Shall we begin?" he asks after slipping the handkerchief away. Then he looks around at the graveyard, the only signs of life are a couple of birds making noise in the trees behind us. "Are we expecting anyone else?" "No, go ahead," I say. My voice is so quiet it's almost lost in the breeze. Diane elbows me. "Your brother," she whispers loud enough for the priest to hear. "Right," I say, trying to sound like I'd forgotten. I hadn't. "Shall we wait?" the priest asks again. "No, go on." He huffs in annoyance, then has to stifle another cough.

My mind is lost as he drones on from his Bible. I don't even remember if my mother was religious. I want to say she wasn't, but how could I have known? I hadn't talked to her except for birthdays and holidays for ten years. Maybe she found God in that time. All alone out here in the middle of nowhere, she'd need someone to talk to, right? "...love is a powerful weapon," the priest drones on. Diane sniffles by my side. It hits me how much I didn't know my mother outside of being a mother.

I didn't know what kind of music she liked, her favorite food, her favorite television shows, movies...I didn't know anything about her. Now I never will because she's lying in a polished, white coffin two feet in front of me, next to a hole in the earth six feet deep. Sometimes, I don't even remember her first name. She's just Mum, never Mom or Mommy. Mother, so prim and proper. The sadness really rolls over me. A tear falls out from behind the cover of my lenses, hits me on my lip, tasting salty, feeling warm. Another one follows and soon I'm sobbing.

Diane wraps her arms around me, pulls me closer. "It's okay," she whispers, but I don't believe her. It will never be okay. My mother is dead and I was a terrible daughter. The priest finishes up with, "Let us go in peace to live out the word of the lord our god," His Bible closes with a sudden, final thump, reminding me of a closing coffin. He walks around the head of the grave and places a hand on my shoulder. With soft eyes and a practiced frown, he says, "I'm sorry for your loss." Me too, I think to myself because I really am. If I could go back in time and fix all of this, I would. "Thank you," Diane says, being my voice of reason. I never got the flowers, I realize. All because Freddy Huber punched me in the face.

The wound throbs at the thought of that bastard. "When you are ready, we will lower her. Take as much time as you need," the priest says. "I'm ready now," I say. "I'm not," a voice calls from behind me. Before I turn around, I already know who it is. Franky Glass. My older brother by five years. He wears a tuxedo, something you might get married in, and he has a bouquet of...you guessed it, roses. Frank lives in some Midwestern town Penicuik, I'm not sure but I am sure he shouldn't have a tan on his face as bright as the sun itself.

I know he's an outdoors man through and through. If I frisked him, I'd probably find a couple of guns, one tucked in his waistband, the other in an ankle holster along with a switchblade or two. He believes in self-defense. He believes in violence. Seriously, go get a time machine and take a look at my childhood. He was always bigger and bolder, always getting in fights and picking on me. Said it would make me tougher, but I think it just gave me nightmares. Really, looking back, I think Frank was bound to serve in the military, bound to make a career out of it.

When he left me and Mother, we unraveled. He was our glue. I would've given anything for him to come back. "Nice of you to show up," I say. "Late." He outstretches his arms. "Little sister, it's been so damn long!" He hugs me and it's both uncomfortable and familiar. Just, like he used to after a punch that was too hard and brought tears to my eyes when we were kids, don't cry, Carly. Mom might hear and whoop both our asses. "How are ya?" He points up at the small cut under my eye and says, "Not too good, I guess," followed by a chuckle. "Not now," I say. "Now's not really the time to play catch-up, is it, Frank?" He looks past me at the coffin. "Right," he says. Then he sees Diane and his jaw drops. "Wow, little sister, you really scored this?" Diane's lip snarls. "Yeah, she did," she says. This is still something I can't comprehend, but yeah, I did. "People?" the priest says. "Shall we continue?" "Yes," I say. Frank answers right after me with a resounding, "No." There's a moment of silence as the priest's eyes dart between us, not knowing who to follow orders from.

The employees stand at each end of the coffin lowering device, their hands hovering above the cranks which will send my mom to her final resting place. "I want to see her again," Frank says. "You could've seen her anytime in the past fifteen years," I say. He ignores me, heads for the coffin, then squats down on the green felt around it. "How the hell do you open this thing?" My hand flies out to stop him. It's not because I know the morticians probably did a terrible job of putting her together, but it's because I might completely dissolve if I have to see her dead. "Leave her alone! All this time and you wanna bother her now?" Frank looks up at me, something he's never done in all thirty-three years of his life, like I've slapped him. "Stop it!" Diane yells.

Her arms are folded across her chest, face growing redder. This is the look I don't like, the one that tells me I better listen or she's going to explode. Frank must see it, too. He may be a giant asshole, but he's no dummy. "Stop it!" she repeats. "You're embarrassing yourselves." I feel the priest's eyes on me, the employees, too. At the same time, I feel God looking down. Maybe even my mom. But the only eyes I care about are Diane's. Frank straightens up, looking at me. "You got a good woman there, little sis. Take good care of her." The comment surprises me. Frank was never too big on sharing compliments; he's more of a jealous-make-excuses-about-why-you're-wrong-and-he's-right kind of guy.

Trust me, you know the type. Has my older brother finally grown up? As if on cue, he walks off, finally sensing he's not welcome. I watch him go for a moment, then I turn to the priest. "Go on." We bury my mom. Me, Diane, a priest, and two overweight cemetery employees whose names I don't remember. The whole time, all I can think about is Kevin Jenkins.

# Chapter Six

I'm not even halfway out of the cemetery when I fish around for the tiny slip of paper I'd pulled free from Mark Hutchins's bulletin board. I dial the number. It rings a few times before someone picks up. A woman. "Hi, this is the Prestonpans Recreation Center. Abby Lang speaking, how may I help you? "Hello, I'm looking for Kevin Jenkins." "Just a moment, please." The receiver clicks as she transfers my call, then the line starts to ring again. "Kevin Jenkins," a deep voice answers on the other line. He sounds tired. "Train hard. Get ripped." "Hey Kevin. It's Carly Glass." Silence. "Carly Glass? No way," he says, a little more perked up. "Yeah, I'm in town for a few days, and I saw your flyer.

I was looking to get in a few good workouts. Pick up some proper training techniques before I drive back to England." "Carly Glass? No shit?" "Yep, it's Carly." Kevin was not always the brightest boy around. I'm at the car now, waiting for Diane who is still back in the funeral home clearing up a few things. "Well, Carly, come on down...let's see, I'm all booked today, but how about tomorrow? Come on down tomorrow at say, no, that's right before the festival, stupid thing." "The festival!" I say. "No, I can do it then. I'm not going, and honestly, between you and me, the fewer people in the gym, the more comfortable I'll be." "Should be deserted around that time, I really don't know why we're open in the first place.

Oh well, I get paid by the hour." He chuckles. "Come in at six sharp, we'll only have about forty-five minutes before the place closes. That cool?" "Perfect." "All right, Carly, I'll get you fixed up." "Thanks, Kevin. Can't wait," I say. There's another uncomfortable silence until Kevin's gruff voice breaks it. "Say, Carly, I heard about your mom. I'm real sorry. It's an awful thing, those deer. Animals have been acting real funny lately. Wrong place " "Don't worry about it," I say, closing my eyes and trying not to think of my mom's coffin covered in dirt. "I'll see you tomorrow." I hang up. Diane is a few steps away, and she grins, trying

28

to comfort me. It's not enough because not even her dazzling smile can stop the tears from coming.

Today is July 3rd. I buried my mother yesterday. I spend the day writing while Diane goes shopping. Most of the shops in the town stay open because they know the festival will bring in a few outsiders (we home-towners know their merchandise is crap). When she gets back, I'm already halfway out the door, heading to the gym. "Be careful," she says, kissing me. "I'll be fine, babe," I say. She grabs my bicep. "I think you're buff enough, misses." I point to my eye. "This says otherwise. I'll be back in about an hour. Maybe we can get a cream cake and watch the fireworks tonight." I caught a glimpse of the high street earlier.

The festival won't officially start until 7:00 p.m., but the people were out and about. Way too many. I recognized a lot of them, but a lot of them, I didn't. All buzzing around, waiting for the fun to start like kids up at the crack of dawn on Christmas morning before their parents even set out the presents. I can't imagine what it'll be like once it actually starts. "I'd like that," Diane says.

I show up to the Prestonpans Recreation Center fifteen minutes early, wearing gym shorts, a plain t-shirt, and a worn-out pair of running shoes which really have no right to be worn-out. A sign on the front door reads:

WILL BE CLOSED, from 7pm SATURDAY, JULY 3rd FOR FESTIVAL. CLOSED ALL DAY SUNDAY, JULY 4th SORRY FOR ANY INCONVENIENCE.

There is an old woman at the front desk who waves hello to me, then takes my name and £8 entry fee. Another younger woman beside her works the phones. She gets up and goes in the back to get Kevin. I see a manager in another room talking on his cell. I don't recognize any of them. Kevin greets me with a big bear hug. He has certainly bulked up. That picture of him was definitely not photo shopped. I may have found a nice career writing (which was something I did secretly all my life) but Kevin completely flipped his life upside down. We make small talk for a bit, and he eventually leads me up a staircase a few paces away from the front doors. This place is huge. I never came here much as a kid, and sometime in high school, they expanded it, adding in three more basketball courts, two racquetball courts, a running track, and an indoor soccer field. "You ready?" Kevin asks.

His gelled hair shines in the fluorescent lighting. He's got a slight tan, not one that looks like he's been in the sun all summer (Prestonpans doesn't get much sun, either) but one that looks like he got from fake UV lights. It's something bodybuilders do for their competitions, I realize, having seen cringe-worthy pictures of ripped dudes all greased up and tan in their bright pink and purple thongs. The thought of Kevin doing something as silly as that brings a bubble of laughter to my lips.

He yells this time, his voice earth-shattering, "I said, are you ready!?" We are standing at the landing at the top of the stairs. About three feet behind me is a thirty-foot roll of jagged steps, and I almost take the tumble. "Y-Yeah," I say. "I guess I am." "I want to hear you roar, Glass!" "Yes! I'm ready!" "Louder," Kevin bellows. "Yes! I'm FUCKING ready!" He slaps me on the chest, and the blow rattles my ribcage. "Good, but don't curse here, It's a family facility." I can feel the blood pumping through my body, the adrenaline, too. I've never been so psyched to workout. "We warm up, then your ass is benching until your tits fall off." "Hey, I thought you said no cursing."

I flash him a weak smile. "I can do what I want. I work here, Glass. Geez, get with the program." The upstairs splits off into two big sections. On the left of the stairs is the weights room, but we go the other way for a ten-minute warmup. Back in England, this would've been my workout. Ten minutes on a stationary bike, and then I'm buying five bucks worth of vending machine junk. Not today. Now I'm warmed up, in the weight room and lying on my back, looking at the white ceiling beams and dark emergency lights.

Kevin is behind me in a tank top, his index fingers lightly touching the barbell as I let it slowly fall to my puffed-up chest. Fans whir in the background. An old Bryan Adams song plays over the loudspeaker. There's a sound of dumbbells clanking together, of shoes thumping a treadmill belt. Then, someone screams, and the weight of the world crushes my chest. Okay, maybe not the weight of the world. It's actually about ninety-five pounds. I'd be okay if Kevin didn't have the attention span of a puppy because he's gone. What am I paying that giant asshole

# Chapter Seven

for? That's right, I'm not. You get what you pay for, I guess. "A little help..." I say, but it comes out like a wheeze.

The scream rips through the air again, this time causing me to turn my head in its direction. It comes for the lower floor, near the front doors. Everyone who is anyone on the second floor weight room hangs over the guardrail to get a look at who or what caused this lady to scream bloody murder. Unfortunately, I'm not one of them. "Anyone? Kevin?" I say. As I strain, the healing cut under my eye threatens to split open. My arms feel like wet noodles. If I push any harder, my head is going to explode. I might be able to roll it off of me, but I doubt it. A lung might be starting to collapse. Each breath is a pain. So, at this point, I'm content with letting myself die.

Who would miss me anyway? Diane...but who else? And Diane missing me isn't a given. I'm still baffled that she agreed to marry me. I mean me, a girl who sits in a dark room typing on a keyboard for a living. A girl who can't fight her own battles. Ten years removed from high school and still the target of bullies like Freddy Huber. Yeah, Diane could've done a lot better than me, that's for damn sure. I give the barbell one last push. Everything I got. A vein pops from my forehead. I feel my face going a devilish red. Heart hammers my sternum, that's good, at least I'm still alive.

Then my vision goes spotty... and finally, black. I'm still here. Not dead yet. Pushing with all of my might. The bar leaves me, the pain with it. I don't know how I did it, but the barbell is hovering above, and I'm hardly pushing. Then I rack it. The whole bench press shakes with the force. My arms drop to my sides like concrete. I exhale, thinking to myself that in a couple months, people will start calling me Rocky Balboa. "You should have a spotter," a girl says. This takes me by surprise. Still lying on the bench, I tilt my head back and see a pair of brown cargo pants and a red shirt. On the shirt is a small white stick figure holding a barbell over their head. I bet she's lifting more than ninety-five pounds, too. On the opposite side of that stick figure is a name tag that reads: ABIGAIL Lang.

She was the one manning the phones when I called yesterday, and now she's the one who's saved my life. I sit up and spin around. It's not an easy task. Again, I'm content with dying right now. "I had a spotter," I say, wiping the back of my iron-smelling hands across my forehead. A polyurethane-sheen of sweat sits on my skin. "But," I point a thumb to my right where the crowd gathers around the guardrail, "he's a little bit busy." I haven't heard a scream in about a minute. "Well, I'd wait until he's not busy before you start your next set." "What happened down there?" I ask. Mainly because I'm too exhausted to get up and go look for myself. Abigail Lang shrugs. "I don't know. I was too busy saving you from being squashed to death."

She puts a hand on one of the twenty-five pound plates, smirks. "By ninety-five pounds, no less." I roll my eyes. This is exactly why I've never wanted to join a gym. Everyone's so judgmental. So what if I can barely bench press half of my body weight? At least I'm trying. "Miss Seton is always screaming at things. She probably saw a spider or something. She loves the attention. Sometimes, I think she thinks that if she screams loud enough, God will finally answer her prayers." A fake chuckle escapes my lips. Her honesty catches me off guard. It's...refreshing. "Right," I say. "Well, thanks, Abigail Lang." "You can call me Abby." "All right, Abby. You can call me Carly Glass." "As in the Carly Glass?" "Yeah, why?" "As in the writer?" I nod. "Yes, the writer." She huffs. "I graduated high school last year. In my last semester, I took Mrs. Beady for English, and man, she wouldn't shut up about you and your books.

We had to read one for an assignment. And she talked about you like you were her favorite child or something. Kinda annoying." I can't help but smile. Beady was tough if memory serves me correctly. A little less tough now that I know she's a fan. "Ah, yeah Mrs. Beady. How is that old hag?" "Still old and haggish," Abby says. We both laugh. Then, she says: "I pictured a girl who could lift a little more than ninety-five pounds, that's all. No offense." "None taken. I thought I could lift more than that, too." "Keep working, and you'll get there," she says. "Thanks " then the scream cuts me off. This one is far worse than all the other screams, and there's a cry of help that follows. It's enough to rattle the mirrors plastered on all of the walls.

One of those screams I'd have a victim in my novels belt out. It gives me the chills. With a little more strength in my body now and being less light-headed, I get up. Abby's eyes are wide, and she starts to shuffle in that direction. "That one sounded a bit more serious," she says. Kevin shifts back and forth. This guy who can probably bench press nine-hundred pounds in comparison to my ninety-five is frightened but rightfully so. As I get closer and see the pale looks on the other people's faces, I start to get this feeling of dread knotting in my chest. I mean, if a guy like Kevin Jenkins can be spooked like he is now, then how will I fare? This thought almost stops me from moving forward until Abby passes. And I can't let her upstage me again.

It's bad enough she had to save my windpipe from being slowly crushed by a barbell. How would I carry on knowing I let myself get spooked by a woman's screams when everyone else wasn't? I walk up to Kevin, standing directly behind him. His large back and wide shoulders make it damn near impossible for me to see past him. Plus his shadow is like a great big oak tree. Against the railing, crowded next to Kevin, is an older fellow drenched in sweat, another man I'd consider a senior citizen with a basketball under one arm, and now, me. The woman below takes to sobbing now. A collective gasp fills the air. I mouth the words: What the fuck? I'm looking at the front doors. There's six of them, mostly glass. Two of them act as the entrance, while the other four, which are separated by a chest-high, wall act as the four exits. They're all about as heavy as the weights upstairs, I swear.

Their glass is spic and span as if they're Windex'd every hour or so. Except for the entrance door. I can't see through it any longer. A smear of red takes up most of the view, like someone covered in paint forgot there was a door there. There's a handprint on the mat about a step in from the door. My eyes follow the trail. On the mat, which houses the Prestonpans Recreation Center's barbell-holding stick figure, is the old woman from the front desk. She clutches what looks like a limp CPR dummy wearing the attire of a police officer. My mind races. I get that spike of blood pressure that comes so often in my life when I'm scared as all hell. "What's going on?" I ask. Nobody answers. The three men up here with me stare with their jaws hanging open. Miss Seton's arms are covered in blood. She's holding the cop's head in her lap, one hand presses against his neck where the bulk of the red seems to flow from. "What the hell?" I say. "It's Burnett," the sweaty, middle-aged guy says. It takes me a moment to realize that this guy speaks the truth. Burnett is covered in so much blood, he's almost unrecognizable. Now it's my turn for my jaw to drop. Since no one is moving, I back away from the guardrail and head down the steps. It's much worse than I expected.

# Chapter Eight

Miss Seton is now wearing as much blood as Burnett. There are tears in her eyes, and she mutters something about God. Praying to him, begging for forgiveness, I don't know. Behind me, I hear the footsteps of the three men from the weight room. And outside, rising high above the blubbering woman and the tennis shoes slapping against rubber-lined steps is the sounds of the Fourth of July parade revving up in the town square not too far away from the Recreation center. The marching band beats their drums, there's rock music playing over loudspeakers, people are talking and cheering, walking down the road to where the action is at, unaware of what chaos is slowly unfolding in the gym.

Miss Seton looks at me, smears of red on her forehead from where she brushed her salt-and-pepper hair out of her face. "Help me," she says. "Please, someone help me." Another employee passes me in a flash. He's a blur of red shirt and khaki pants. He's probably pushing sixty, graying hair, clean-shaven face and a neck like a bullfrog. "Oh, God, Fiona," he says. "What happened?" She babbles on for a moment before saying, "I-I don't know. I saw him walking toward the entrance, holding his neck. He almost collapsed, but I grabbed him and got him inside.

He was talking, and when we got through the doors, he fell. I couldn't hold him anymore." Abby Lang disappears behind the front desk. She's gone for a few seconds before she's back with a stack of bleach-white towels, the kind they have at the front of the weight room so you can clean off the machines when you're done using them. The older guy grabs a handful and stuffs them against the Officer's neck. "We gotta call someone," he says, and before he's done with the sentence, the towels soak through with red. He grabs more, jams them against the others. This is when I unfreeze. I run to the phone since my iPhone is baking in the glove box of my rented car.

For this first workout, I wanted total focus. No music. No small talk. Just me and the weights. Isn't that just the stupidest thing? Yeah, like I said before, hindsight is 20/20. I grab the office phone and dial 999. The old woman, Fiona Seton, starts screaming again. Tears fall from her eyes, slicing the drying blood on her cheeks like some kind of fucked-up Moses parting the red sea. Her screams are even worse this close. I have to plug one of my ears to listen for the voices assuring me it will be okay on the other end. It rings once, twice, then dead. A semblance of a busy signal, then fuzz. I try again. This time, I don't even get a ring. It's the "We're sorry, the number you have called cannot be reached. Please hang up and try again" lady voice we all love to hate. I'm about to try for a third time because the third time's the charm and all when I hear the Officer's voice through my plugged up ear.

He doesn't talk so much as croak. "There...there's so many of them. I-It just happened so fast..." "What happened so fast, Officer? What?" the man holding the bloody towels asks. "It's the e-end of the world." Hearing the Officer's gurgling voice say that sends shivers up my back. I blink a few times, thinking this will be a dream and I'll wake up in bed. That doesn't happen. Obviously it's not the end of the world. If I look out the window, I can see some of the festival stragglers, wearing silly looking hats, dressed in the patriotic red, white, and blue and other costumes. No, it's not the end of the world. The whole town is out there enjoying the world right now.

This must be some kind of sick prank. Kevin put it together to get back at me for not keeping in touch for the last decade. He knows I write horror novels. How funny would it be to prank that guy who writes about zombies and werewolves? Freakin' hilarious. "Call someone!" the man holding the towels says to me. He turns, and I see the worry on his face. His eyes are glassy. Maybe he'll cry. Maybe he's on the verge of a heart attack. I don't know. Pinned to his chest opposite of the barbell-holding stick figure is his name tag that reads: MANAGER and below it, BOBBY LAVENDER. Something about his expression tells me he can't fake this. "Get an ambulance out here right now!" he snaps again. This time, he bares his teeth. And the intensity in his wrinkled forehead spurs me to dial 999 for the third time, prank or not. I get nothing.

A dead line. "Phone's down," I say. "I tried three times." It's not a good enough answer for the guy. "Try a goddamn fourth time!" he shouts. The boom in his voice shakes more sobs and tears out of Miss Seton. I pick up the receiver for the fourth time but pause when something catches my eye outside. I see more of the festival-goers coming this way, not toward the square but toward the rec center. This street is a dead end, all forest and steel barriers. This has to be a prank. It doesn't make sense, but I see it. I see the top hats, the kids holding tiny flags, more and more people. Ahead of them all is another cop.

This one is a woman, and she has sleek-black hair that catches the sun. She's limping, laboring over toward the rec like a drunk. I chuckle at the idea of the cops celebrating instead of doing their jobs. I really couldn't blame her if she pounded a few beers while on patrol. I'd do the same thing. It's all part of the show, I think to myself. Back to the phone. I punch in 999 again. Get nothing. Just got to go with it until one of them jumps up and yells GOTCHA! "Not working," I say.

Tony Lavender growls at me, then sweeps his gaze over the small crowd of onlookers. "Someone use their cell phone. Come on! Quick!" Kevin Jenkins has an iPhone in a case wrapped around his massive bicep. His fingers work their way inside until he pulls it free. With one clean rip, he disconnects the headphones that hang from his arm like a spider web. I see him fiddle with the screen for a moment then put the phone up to his ear. Let me guess, "No answer. Just keeps ringing and ringing," he says. Of course there's no answer. Yawn. Abby Lang pulls her phone out of her back pants pocket. It has a pink case with a big blue flower on the back. A few seconds later, she says the same thing: "No answer."

I clear my throat and walk out from behind the desk. "Looks like another cop is on her way down," I say, then under my breath: "As if on cue." I'm smiling. "I guess I'll wave her down." Fiona and Tony both follow my pointing finger. "No, I'll do it," he says, his voice curt. All part of the show. "Oh thank you, God," Tony says. He grabs Fiona's hand and guides it to the dripping-red towels. "Just another minute, Miss Seton, and then it'll be okay." The door squeaks as the hinges open. He's in the lobby, now, poking his head out of the second set of doors that lead outside.

I hear his voice; it's muffled but clear. The music comes in louder. "Help us, Becky. Burnett is hurt!" Tony yells. The cop outside is nothing more than a human-shaped blur through the two layers of glass, but I see her stop. She doesn't answer with her voice and turns her head slow and deliberate at the sound of Tony. Tony leaves the lobby completely and goes outside. His pace is frantic, again moving faster than he should be able to. The female cop picks up her speed. It's a beautiful day outside. The sun shines down on the parking lot, sparsely populated by the few cars that didn't go up to the square for the festival.

Rays catch the windshields and gleam off the polished metal door handles. But the sun also illuminates the cop's face. She might've been pretty once, but she's not pretty anymore. My first thought is they really went all out with the fake blood and prosthetics. There must be a camera crew around here somewhere. More blood stains her pale-blue uniform. She limps like she's hurt. A spike of fear hits me. What if this isn't a prank? What if this is real? I start backing away from the door, unable to pry my eyes from her. "Easy, buddy," Kevin Jenkins says in his deep voice.

I turn to look at him. He pats me on the shoulder with enough force to break my clavicle. I'm expecting the GOTCHA at any moment, but everyone is too busy watching the scene unfold. There's the sweaty dude, whose shirt is so soaked through, I can see his nipples; there's Fiona Seton leaning up against the glass divider with the bloody

Burnett on her lap; Abby Lang holding her pink cell phone; a few other people dressed in their workout gear, the old man, a black guy, a high school-aged janitor dressed in a blue version of the employee uniform. "What's all over her face?" Abby asks. No one answers. Blood, I say. "Blood because she's just took a bite out of Burnett or some other poor, unknowing bastard." I laugh. Everyone gives me uncomfortable looks. "This is priceless!" Abby walks closer to the window. Kevin moves forward too. I catch the scent of his Old Spice deodorant as he goes past me. Then, Abby screams almost too real to be faked.

Outside, Tony hits the pavement on his knees. His body turns to us. The woman cop has raked him across the face, and now he holds the wound. I can see the blood seeping between his tightly-knit fingers and more dripping from hers, but I didn't see the hit. The cop lunges again, this time missing. Tony gets back up on his feet. I hear him say the cop's name: "Becky?" and it comes out like a question, like he's stunned this woman just bitch-slapped him and they're going off script.

A glare of sunlight catches her eyes. He's backing away, one arm still on the gash. Maybe this isn't right. I push through the doors and into the lobby. I'm going to put a stop to it, let them know I know it's a prank and they can stop their stupid act now before I lose my mind. The sun blazes against my skin. To my right is a flag pole. The wind blows, fabric snaps, and metal cables smack against each other. With the wind, comes a scent. It's bad enough for me to raise my t-shirt over my nose. It's a smell of death, of road kill baking in the sun on the side of the highway. It only adds to my doubt. "All right, guys, I get it. You got me, really funny. Ha-ha," I say through the cotton. There's a lot of fake blood.

Tony hesitates at first then shuffles toward me like he's running for his life. The cop is left behind for the moment, but she's determined. "What?" Tony says. "What is going on? Help me!" Nope, no GOTCHA. Not yet. How much longer will they drag this out? I keep the door open, seeing him in the sunlight. Really seeing him. The greatest makeup artist in the world couldn't do what's happened to Tony's face. I try to piece it together. Maybe he's wearing two layers of prosthetics, one with the gash covered by one that looks freaky, but that seems like a lot of work to prank someone like me.

It just looks so real, too. Fresh blood sputters from the claw-like gashes across his eye, even the eyebrow has been raked off. This can't be a prank, it just can't. I'm witnessing mutilation. Despite having grown up a bit since my last stint in Prestonpans, I almost shit my pants as the realization of this situation hits me. Tony reaches the flag pole. I lean forward and try to grab his hand. Even the hand that's not over the ripped flesh on his face is splattered with blood. He's looking over his shoulder at the shuffling cop when I make a connection. I pull him into the lobby. The door doesn't slam shut. It's one of those hydraulic doors that are heavy as hell to open and take forever to close.

We head for the second set of doors where Kevin stands, propping it open. Tony trips and falls. He's so heavy he takes me down with him. I hear hinges squeak. Everyone's gasps and screams are amplified. There's a faint gurgling noise behind me. It's what I'd call a death rattle, and I know it's coming from Becky. I know she's made her way into the lobby, but I can't help but look. Her eyes are sunken in, not freaky eyes at all. In fact, I'd say they're dead eyes. Skin, too. It's the color of Swiss cheese. The blood around her mouth is fresh and wet, not even close to drying, and now, I realize, not even close to being fake.

She moans again, opens her eyes wider. They're yellow, almost glowing. "Oh fuck," I say as she lunges forward. Kevin grabs my right arm. I'm still holding onto Tony's slick, bloody hand. He's screaming. The hand's too wet. I slip off. Kevin drags me over the lobby's carpet. My ass burns through my shorts. Despite all his strength, I hear Kevin grunting. "Lock the doors!" he screams. Now I'm sliding across the tile. "Tony," I say. But it's too late. He's in the lobby. One of his shoes flies up to meet the cop's face. It doesn't even phase her. She raises her hands, hands that look more like gnarled tree branches.

She doesn't have a carving knife, she's not a bodybuilder or particularly strong-looking, she's just determined. She digs into the soft flesh of Tony's stomach. He doesn't stand a chance.

# Chapter Nine

I've never seen anything like this. This is worse than anything my writer brain could cook up. Yet, here I am on the floor, a group of mewling, frightened people behind me as we watch Tony getting his stomach ripped apart. All notions of this being a prank have completely gone out the window along with my breakfast. Becky, this once officer of the law, is too distracted with her meal to look up at us. We watch her feast like she's a zoo animal. I want to crawl away, I want to stop looking, but I can't. Becky is a zombie. It's that simple. It's that complicated. She has a hankering for human flesh and organs, and seeing her do this is almost hypnotic.

My third published novel was a zombie story. It was called The Death Slayer. I had a blast writing it, but it was not well-received by the critics. They said it was too "genre-bending" and "all over the place," whatever the hell that means, it was a zombie novel, cut me some slack. Anyway, the point I'm trying to make is that I recognize this, perhaps more so than a normal person would. In a sense, I've lived it before with Carly the Death slayer, my novel's macho, reserved, blood-covered main character. I know the signs, the mannerisms, and weaknesses of the dead. For a second, this gives me hope.

Watch any zombie movie and you know you have to take out their brains. Sharp objects, bullet to the head. Decapitation, easy, Simple. But Tony is still alive and he's yelling worse than any dying man I've brought forth from my imagination to the page ever could, and all my confidence deflates. "Someone help him!" Fiona Seton says. "She's killing him!" Worse than that, she's eating him...alive. Tony's insides are now outside. The cop's face is mostly blood. She brings up some kind of organ out of Tony's open stomach. The tissue stretches as she pulls it up to her mouth, finally snapping free with a red mist. Tony's screams are dying with him.

His head lolls. For a second, I think our eyes meet, but they just roll to the back of his head, exposing the whites. I look away. Abby Lang has a key in her hand attached to a string which is attached to her belt loop. She slides the key into each handle, turns it with a heavy click. Her other hand hovers over her eyes, so she's not tempted to see her boss get devoured. Then she hops over the glass divider, lands right in front of me and locks the last two doors. She lingers for a second, closes her eyes, shakes her head. "Here," she says, offering me a hand. I take it and it's about as sweaty as the middle-aged guy's t-shirt. "It's not going to be enough," I say to her, then raise my hands. "There's more coming. We're trapped. There's too many. When they group up, they're stronger and more deadly than any military." I'm babbling now. "What?" Fiona Seton says, then sets her head in her hands, rocks back and forth. "Zombies?" I ignore her. The festival. Something had to have happened at the festival." The wall of the undead makes their way down the small hill of the recreation center's entrance.

They move just like the cop did. Like I said, there's too many, or else I could run. They may be slow, but what they lack in speed, they make up for in numbers. "See that?" I say, pointing to them. "Fuck," Kevin says. "How do you know they're...they're like that?" Abby asks. "Look at them! Just look!" I say. I step over Burnett. "Kevin, help Miss Seton move this guy out of the way. We need to start barricading the doors." "Barricade them? They're locked!" the sweaty-guy says standing next to Kevin. "Besides, it's just one person. I can get past her." He moves forward, but Kevin puts a big, meaty arm in his way, then shakes his head. "You walk out there, you're dead, Pat," he says. "Locked, yeah," I say. "But they're all glass.

It's not gonna take much for them to break through once they pile up." "He's right," Abby says. "For your own good," Kevin says. He bends down to pick Burnett up. Miss Seton has the towels wrapped around his wound like a scarf. The bleeding has mostly stopped, yet Kevin's face is like a man's who stepped in dog shit. "Oh screw that," the sweaty guy named Pat says. "You can't hold me here against my will." I point out the window toward the growing crowd of shambling festival-goers. "They can," I say. "Where do I put him?" Kevin asks.

It takes me a moment to realize what he's asking. My mind races with fear, with confusion. "We can't keep him here," I say. "A bite is fatal. Look at his neck, someone took a chunk out of it." "How do you know it's fatal?" Abby asks. "I don't know for sure, but why take a chance?" I say. "Because it's a human life," Kevin says. "Because it's Burnett, for crying out loud!" "What do you suggest?" Abby says. "We throw him outside?" They are as confused and scared as I am, and Kevin is right. It is a human life. What if I'm wrong? What if the bite doesn't turn him? I can't live with that on my conscious. "Do you have a room that locks, preferably one with a window so we can look in on him?" I ask. Abby ponders the question. "The athletic room locks, but I don't think there's a window." "That'll do for now," I say. "Here, follow me," Abby says, looking to Kevin.

They go back behind the desk, then disappear into the shadowy corridors. I lend a hand to help Miss Seton up. She's an older woman. Fifty, maybe pushing sixty with a homely face, the kind of face that would welcome a total stranger into her home for a glass of water, and freshly-baked cookies. She won't be much help in barricading the door, but she'll be even less help if she's just sitting here in the way. She takes my hand, tears in her eyes, no smile on her face. A blank slate, A woman who's seen too much in too short a time. "This is God's wrath.

This is His fury," she says. Her voice is chilling. Still, I shake my head, do my best to ignore her. We walk past the front desk, under the walkway that leads to the second floor weight lifting room, across the track and into the cafeteria area. There is three Coca-Cola vending machines, a snack machine, and a coffee machine. The lights are bright, like hospital bright. Floors are spotless and shining. I pull out her chair for her, which slides easily along the tile, and she sits down.

No-one else is in the cafeteria area. "Just stay right there, and I'll go get you some water and fresh rags," I say. She nods. I walk back to the doors. The festival-goers hit the outside glass. Thunk thunk thunk. Heads and faces smeared with blood. Others totter back and forth, bumping into each other like aimless cattle. On the floor in the lobby, Becky has her face in Tony's stomach, almost buried completely.

I think of a pie eating contest in hell and what it would be like, and the only image that pops into my head is what I'm seeing right now. I pause at the front door, not looking at the tragedy occurring in front of me, but looking past it. There's more than I thought. A lot more. They move with the mentality of a hungry pack of wolves. I just want to survive. I want to go back to England. It's in this lull I remember Diane's not here. She could be back at the motel. She could be dead. Or she could be a zombie. God, the thought is enough to make me double over. I feel tears stinging my eyes. To think of her dead or as a zombie, it's just too much. She's the reason I am the woman that I am today, the reason I'm no longer scared, the reason I'm moderately successful. Not Prestonpans. Not my mother or my long-lost father. Diane. She's also the reason why I can't lie down and curl up in to a little ball. My fiction has become a reality, that's true. Carly Death slayer wouldn't quit, and neither will Carly Glass. I straighten up and wipe the tears away with the back of my hand.

Two men carry over a cracked-leather couch near the stairs to the second floor. They set it longways against the four doors that comprise the exit. One of them, a black man with a basketball player's physique, drops his end with a clatter. The other, the young janitor kid does the same. "Aw, what the fuck?" the black guy says. "She's eating his throat, man. Oh hell no." Another man, old, but in decent shape, wearing a basketball jersey with the number 18 hanging off the back in frays, says, "Don't look." It's too late not to look.

You see it once, it burns into your brain. They both know it because they're quiet now, and they're still staring. It's at this moment that I notice the silence in the building. Like everything clicked off at once. The air conditioner isn't humming. The lights flicker. My eyes go up to the ceiling. From the ceiling, hangs large lights in rows of ten or maybe fifteen. They're like spotlights hung upside down. Each light clicks off one after the other until the only light in the place comes from the sun outside. Then the air starts to blow, though not as strongly.

From where I stand I can see the red glow of the Coca-Cola vending machine. A few lights stuck on the walls around the building turn on. Back up lights. An emergency generator. This is even worse, it means the power went out. Maybe around the whole block or the whole town...hell, maybe the whole world. Diane huddled up in a ball in the pitch-black crosses my mind, her hands over her ears to block out the moaning of the dead.

I grind my teeth. Can't let this get me down anymore. Looking outside, I mentally prepare my escape route. There is may be a hundred people jammed together in the rec's small parking lot. It's only a fraction of what the festival usually gets. Miss Seton will have to wait. I turn and run to grab the other couch. Resting on the brick wall is the sweaty middle-aged guy. He's scrolling through his iPhone with a twisted look on his face, mashing his fingers against the touchscreen and muttering, "C'mon, you goddamned piece of shit. C'mon!" "If the phone lines are down, I think the cell towers would be, too," I say. He ignores me. "I'm Carly." It comes out stilted and awkward. I've never been too good at talking with people I don't know. "We could use a little help." "Yeah, yeah," he says. I linger, expecting more. He moves the phone away from his squinted eyes and says, "Damn it." "What's your name?" "Pat. And no, I'm not helping. I don't plan on sticking around." "Believe me, I want to leave, too. I got a fiancé, but it's too dangerous, " He cuts me off. "Yeah, yeah, save it, kid.

I get that you're scared. I just don't give a shit." He's frowning. It reminds me of someone, but I don't know who. "Whatever," I say, turning toward the other couch. "What-ever," Pat echoes, trying to mimic my tone. I scoff, then the black guy and I lift up the other couch and drag it toward the two entrance doors. Abby shows up with a cart full of weight plates. She wheels them over to me. I stack forty-five pounders near the legs of the couch so none of those things can push it over the tile. I don't know how well it's going to work, but it's all we have.

The old man comes back. He has jump ropes draped around his neck like scarves. Abby smiles, takes the jump ropes, and wraps them around the handles of each pair of doors. It's not much, but Abby must've been a girl scout because she ties a complicated knot that I know I'd never be able to untie without a pair of hedge clippers. Abby looks pale and near death. "My mom," she says. "Is she going to be okay?" I nod. "Yeah, she is. Don't worry." I've always been a good liar. Sometimes, I can even convince myself.

So I have no problem convincing her. Truth is, I don't know if anyone is going to be okay. Not even Diane. I push the thought away again. She smiles, then goes back to tying her jump rope knots. Most of the doors are covered by various work-out equipment. Through a crack between one of the couches and the glass divider, I see our ravenous cop has finished with Tony's stomach because most of it is gone.

Now she works on his face. Bits have been chewed away already. His teeth stretch up to his nose with the absence of his upper lip. One of his eyes hangs from the socket near his ear on a tangled optic nerve. Most of the carpet is stained red. There's blood on the community news board. A sign for a lost kitten is almost completely drenched, soggy and falling from its thumbtack. There's another scream from inside of the rec. Not Miss Seton's. The scream came from behind the front desk. It's Kevin. Burnett must've turned already. We've been infiltrated. We're screwed. I turn to run toward my old friend. Abby Cage says, "Wait up!" from behind me.

The offices behind the desk are a maze. Sounds seem to echo off every wall. I see a ray of sunlight cast across the hallway floor. A blast of heat hits me. The screams are louder. I reach a white room. The Officer is passed out on the table, bloody towels still stuck to the wound on his neck. Every few seconds, he turns his head back and forth and clamps his eyes shut tight, wrinkling the skin, making him look much older. He hasn't turned. He's not locked in, either. I pull the door closed, hoping it locks automatically, knowing it doesn't.

Where is Kevin? I don't linger much longer. I follow the heat and dwindling sunlight streaming in. Around the corner at the end of the hall, an emergency exit is open. One of the zombies has Kevin's arm in her blood-slimy hands. Yellow eyes bear into my soul, freezing me to the spot. "Help me!" Kevin says. "Don't just stand there. Help me!"

# Chapter Ten

I unfreeze, but the woman doesn't seem to notice. Instead, she just opens her mouth. Blood lines her teeth. Clumps of saliva hang from her lips. She moans like a person suffering from the worst case of the flu. I'm scared as all hell, but I plunge my hand in the tangle of limbs. For a second, I go numb all over my body. I think of Diane. I think of the life we could've had together. The kids, the house, the vacations, the white-picket fence. Then my fingers close around the woman's arm. Her skin is burning hot. I pull with all my might. Kevin breaks free, falls to the ground and starts scrambling away. Abby grabs him around the waist and pulls, a futile effort. That's all well and good except now I'm the zombie's sole focus.

I try to let go, to turn and run, but she weighs about a thousand pounds. Dead weight. We topple over. I hit the carpet with a lung-exploding thud. Spit drips onto my cheek. I smell that road kill scent of death. "No!" Abby screams. I hear what sounds like a stampede coming for me.

Then something whizzes by my face. It's a size fifteen Nike. The toe connects with the zombie's face. A few teeth fly out of her mouth along with her whole body being lifted off of me. She goes crashing into the wall, half hanging outside into the beautiful July day. I get up fast. It's times like these I wish I was stronger. Which is why, I was in the gym in the first place. Losing most of my life, being picked on and ridiculed in high school can have a damaging effect on the kid, one that bleeds into his adult life. I, Carly Glass, am a prime example. "Are you all right? Are you hurt?" Abby asks me.

I nod, wiping my face off with the bottom of my shirt. I am dazed. "Holy shit, did I kill her?" Kevin says. "Fuck, I killed her." His voice is usually deeper than the ocean, but now he sounds like a kid in the throes of voice-changing puberty. "No, they are already dead," I say. "We have to remember that." "Oh God, I'm a murderer," he says, then turns back to look at me. "This never happened. Anyone asks, this never happened." The zombie's up against the wall like a crumpled piece of trash.

There's a checkmark branded on her forehead. More blood runs near the wound it's her blood this time. Abby echoes my thoughts. "I-I think she is dead..." "We need to be thorough," I say. "Go get me scissors, or a knife. Something sharp." "Uh, guys..." Abby says. Too late. She points to the crumpled woman. I turn to follow her gaze. That death rattle fills the air. A hand reaches out to grab at us. Kevin is quick, but I'm not. That's what sitting around playing video games and writing gets me. One hand grabs my ankle, then the other wraps around my calf.

I try to shake her off me. It doesn't work. Instead, I fall to the floor. Kevin is on me, about to yank me to safety like he did in the lobby. But the zombie is determined, and apparently, hungry. Two gunshots ring out in the small hallway. My eardrums feel like they're about to explode. I scream, closing my eyes but don't hear myself. When I open them, Burnett stands shakily, the towels still wrapped around his neck. He holds his gun out in front of him. A wisp of smoke flutters into the air and his arms wobble one last time before he lets them drop to his side.

This dead woman is now missing a chunk of her head. Blood drenches the pale walls; it rolls down the cracked emergency exit door in round droplets. "Now, she's definitely dead," I say to Kevin. Burnett takes a breath then promptly falls down on the floor at Abby's feet. She yelps. The gun bounces off the carpet and rolls toward me. I pick it up. Kevin grapples the Officer, starts taking him to the athletic trainer's room, leaving us. Abby's face is a mask of tears. She's red. Her hair is no longer in a tight ponytail, strands hang over her forehead into her eyes.

I don't know what to say or do to comfort her. Really, what are my options? So I don't say anything at all. I go toward the emergency exit. "Help me move her outside before more show up," I say. Abby nods.

I grab her feet. Abby grabs her arms. "This is not how I expected my day to go," Abby says. "Why couldn't this crap wait for another month and a half? "What's in a month and a half?" I ask, grunting with the zombie's weight. "When, I move out of this hell-hole." We go through the door. I drop my end of the dead woman.

We are too late. Part of the crowd has already moved from the front to the side where this emergency exit exits to. They are drawn by sound. Basic primal instincts keep them going. What sound is better at attracting the dead than freaking gunshots? I don't intend to get devoured today, so I pull the pistol out of the waistband of my gym shorts. How hard can it be to shoot a gun? I've never done it, not except for video games when there's assisted aiming and, most importantly, no consequences. So I pull the trigger, unsure of where to aim, just knowing it's into the crowd. When the gun cracks, I pull the trigger a second time for safe measure. "Oh, God," Abby says from behind me in a muted voice. The nearest green dumpster is drenched in brains. Spots of red and bits of flesh stick to the metal bin like paint.

One of the dead is down while the others trample its lifeless corpse. The other shot went wide, hitting a young man in the chest, driving him back a foot, but not doing much to slow him down. The sight sickens me and excites me at the same time. I raise the gun, not knowing how many bullets are left, aiming at the closest zombie, which is a man in a tank top. I imagine its Freddy Huber, my vivid imagination kick-starting. Hopefully this will soften the guilt. I don't get to pull the trigger. Abby grabs the back of my arm and pulls me inside before the dead wash over me. Another five seconds and I would've been a meal. She slams the door, pulls out her trusty key, and locks it. "What are you doing? Trying to get us killed?" she says. "If they get in, we're dead.

You said it yourself!" I say nothing. I know my reasons. Crazy as they maybe. I thought I could clear a path, I thought I could get to Diane. Kevin is standing around the corner he holds a broken broom handle, muscles flexed. He relaxes a bit when he sees us, but still somehow looks like King Kong. "The Officer," he says, "he's mumbling, and he's talkin' about the end of the world again. I-I think he's gonna die."

Burnett does look like he's going to die soon, and there's nothing I can do to help him. The room is quiet, except for the slightest breeze of cool air escaping from the small whole under a sink counter. Cool air that does nothing for us. The power is still off. Everything is running on the backup generator, and the temperature suffers from it. Burnett smells the way my grandpa smelt in his hospital bed three days after his stroke, the day he died. His eyes are wide open. He studies Abby, Kevin, and me like we're works of art on display at some museum.

He looks at us, but I'm not sure if he really sees us. "It...it hurts," he says. "She bit me and...and it hurts really bad," I lean closer, part of me still thinking this is just some cruel prank. I'm covered in blood enough as it is so it doesn't matter to me as I reach out to move the towels off his neck. They don't come easily. It's like they're glued to his skin. Dried blood snags on the fabric. Burnett winces as I pry it free. A ripping noise fills my ears, and I smell rotting flesh. Old, spoiled chicken breasts you forgot in your car on a ninety-degree day after a trip to the supermarket. I'm curious. I want to see if it looks like I'd imagined, like the bites in my zombie novel. But I'm also disgusted. Let's call it morbid curiosity. Abby squirms and shuffles away behind me. Kevin makes an "Ew" sound. "They don't die..." he says.

The wound is gruesome. "S-She was just a kid!" Burnett screams, and he does half of a sit-up with the shake in his voice. "She was just a kid, and I shot her...three times. B-But she k-kept coming. She wouldn't die. All I wanted to do was get through that damn festival. I didn't want to kill anyone. What was I supposed to do?" I know how he's feeling because I am in the same boat. Burnett is a danger as long as he's left alive. I will have to put him down before he can turn. I don't want to. I have to. Burnett's eyelids flutter. I see the pain on his face, hear it in his voice. "She died...they all died. I felt their pulses. They weren't breathing. Then...then they rose. All of them. She bit me.

The little girl bit me. Her teeth were like...were like a bear trap. I couldn't get her off of me. I-I panicked. Then she bit Fred and Stacy. The florist lady. Mayor Gorman got it too. I couldn't do my j-job, I had to...had to run. There were too many. The whole town...dead. Dead!" He screams and shakes, pain wracking through his body. "It's okay," I say. But somehow the way Burnett describes it is worse than I thought. It's not okay. This is real, and it's not okay. From the hallway, bangs come from the other side of the walls, almost like gunshots.

It's the zombies outside, my mind's eye imagines Fred and Stacy, Mayor Gorman, and whoever else was bit. They want in; they want us. "Everything all right?" the old man says from the front desk. "Not really," Kevin says, poking his head around the door frame into the hallway. "What the fuck's goin on back there, y'all? I heard gunshots." "Yeah, you did," I holler. "Kevin, go let them know what's going on." He does.

Then I look at Abby, and in a quieter voice, I say: "How many other doors are there? How many other ways can those things get in?" She cups her left elbow with her right hand, looks up to the ceiling. "Uh, let's see...there is the front doors, but we got those barricaded. This exit, which I locked, exits on the opposite side of the building near the basketball courts, the other near the indoor soccer field, and the loading bay. Yeah, I think that's it," she says. They all lead to a place too close to the front of the building which kills my delusions of escape. "Are they all locked?" I ask. "Should be." "Should be? Go check," I say. There's venom in my voice, but I'm sorry, I don't want to end up like Burnett or Tony.

I don't want to be shot three times and still be alive and craving human flesh. Abby leaves. It's me and Burnett in the small athletic training room. Every time he squirms, the legs of the wooden table creak under his weight. I put my hand on his, and tell him it's going to be okay. He shakes his head. "It burns, son. You have to help me. Please," he says. This man is beyond saving. He wouldn't make the trip to the ambulance even if the damn bus backed up over all those freaks outside, crashed through the building, and opened their doors right here in this very room.

So I lie again. "It's going to be okay. We're gonna get you some help." He scrunches up his face. His eyes take on the same look of a deflated balloon. Then the look passes. He's almost serene-looking. "Just shoot me kid. Just s-shoot me in the fuckin head." My eyes drift toward the gun I have in my waistband, his gun and I think about it, like really think about it. I know where this is going, this day, this night. We aren't going to get any help unless we help ourselves, and the odds are stacked against us.

He shudders again, creaking the table with the movement. It's like the scream of a small animal caught in the spokes of a bike tire. I can't take it. "Please, kid. Please. It burns." The screams get louder now. My head pounds with the force of the now-deceased marching band drum. I got to get out of here, got to get away from this guy. "We're going to get you help," I say. "I promise, Officer Burnett." But even a deaf man could hear the lie in my voice. He shakes again, this time bringing his arms up and crossing them over his body as if trying to keep himself together.

It's a sad sight to see a man at the end of his rope, begging for death. I turn to leave, to not put myself through this any longer. I am no Carly Death Slayer. I am Carly Glass, and it's so much harder to kill someone who isn't already dead. I leave him there, rocking back and forth and, screaming in pain, locking and closing the door behind me. "Please kill me...pleaseeeeee."

# Chapter Eleven

The front doors are secured. I see through a crack in the stacked equipment and couches that most of the people outside haven't figured out how to work a door-knob, and haven't even broken into the lobby yet. But there's more than before. They moan and death, rattle together so it's loud enough to hear on the inside. Hands and faces press against the glass. I see teeth, yellow eyes, disfigured, faces. Soon, they will break that glass, and soon they'll be closer to getting in. The old man, dressed in his basketball jersey, stands against the waist-high brick wall that separates the running track from the waiting area opposite the front desk. He shakes his head, runs a hand through his white hair. I watch this from the door that leads to the front desk.

He doesn't see me, either. His lips move silently and he looks up to the high ceiling with its dimmed lights and he does the sign of the cross. God can't help us now. "Give us the gun!" someone yells. My head snaps to the left, where the crowd of survivors is grouped in the cafeteria area. It's the sweaty guy who's yelling. Pat is his name, and I can already tell he's a total asshole, the type of guy who bullies people thirty years out of high school and cheats on his wife when the opportunity presents itself. I could be wrong.

Kevin towers over the man by at least nine inches, and he probably weighs about fifty pounds more, all muscle. Yet, Kevin is pressed up against the door that leads behind the food stand. He has his hands up as if to say he's innocent. Pat points a finger at his face. "I don't have it," Kevin says. "Oh, please, gentlemen, this is not the time to fight. Please, for the love of God, settle down," Miss Seton says. I forgot about Miss Seton, but she looks like she found her way to the women's bathroom to clean up. I know Pat is playing with fire. Kevin is liable to snap at any moment, and in the process, snap Pat's neck. We don't want that. There's enough death outside. I jog over. My lungs burn from the short trip. I really should've started this whole workout thing a long time ago.

In the cafeteria, is everyone but the old man. Miss Seton, Kevin, the black guy whose name I think is George, Pat, and the young man who I think is a janitor. Abby is off locking the doors. "Hey, I have the gun," I say, as I round the corner of the cafeteria, as the rubber flooring of the track breaks into white and gray tile. Pat stops pointing his finger at Kevin, and wheels around to look at me. "Hand it over, son," he says, doing his best to impersonate a fatherly figure. "No." "Goddamn it, kid, if you don't hand it over a lot of bad shit is going to happen." "A lot of bad shit already happened," I say.

And I'm going to make sure there'll be no more. Everyone's eyes blaze into me. It's like I'm on a stage and they're the crowd. "Someone who can handle a weapon should be in charge of it," the janitor says. He's leaning on a cart chock full of toilet paper, fresh-white rags, and various other cleaning supplies, below the supplies is an ancient radio, beaten and cracked. Maybe he's twenty, but I'd say he's still in high school, judging by the scraggly patches of hair on his face. Not too much younger than me, but I feel like I really grew up in the last half-hour. "What makes you think I don't know how to handle a gun?" I say to the janitor kid, taking a step closer.

His name tag reads: Ryan Peterson. "Ain't you that writer? Carly, something? I seen your picture in the paper a couple years ago." "Yeah, so what?" "Why would we expect you to know how to handle a piece?" "Ryan," Miss Seton hisses. "Don't talk like them." The black guy's eyes widen. "Uh, excuse me? What's that supposed to mean?" Ryan ignores them both. Abby walks in from the other side of the cafeteria, where the basketball courts stand empty and dark, devoid of all bouncing balls. "He handled it just fine," she says. "That's what you were doing outside? Target practice?" Pat asks.

His nostrils flare on each syllable, and he's turning a shade of red I associate with the blood on Officer Burnett's neck. "I was saving our asses," I say. "Hand it over, son. You aren't fit to handle a weapon," Pat says. "And you are?" I ask. "What do I have to go on to believe you're our best choice?" He doesn't answer, just tilts his head at me. "We have bigger problems than who gets the gun," I say. "You may be right. Just another reason why you give the gun to a true adult," Pat says. "This isn't one of your fantasy stories. This is real life." He turns to the others, who are all bunched together. "Obviously Carly here has a big imagination. She can't even separate fact from fiction!" A couple people nod in agreement.

The others stare with blank looks on their faces. Faces full of fear and uncertainty. They don't look bright, but they're the realists. I know because I'm one of them. "Come on, man," George says, then shakes his head. "We don't need all this negativity." I get an idea. Obviously I'm not going to reason with Pat. He's one of those "I'm so much better than you" dick-weeds all because he makes six figures a year and wears a suit and tie to work. I point at George. "Here, you take the gun." His eyes grow wide. "Me? C'mon, man, quit playin." I reach into my waistband, pull the gun free. "You really gonna argue with the dude who has a gun?" I flash him a smile to show him I'm not totally crazy, but thinking from his point of view, I probably look almost as crazy as dead people craving human flesh.

"Take it," I say. Pat's shaking next to him. He's not scared; he's just royally pissed. "Why?" George says. "Because I'm black." That catches me off-guard. "Race has nothing to do with it. You're an outside party. You don't lean one way or the other if you catch my drift. You're middle ground." "Then give it to Miss Seton here," he says. The smile on my face evaporates. "She won't take it," I say. "Nuh-uh," Miss Seton echoes. He chuckles, nodding his head. "You're right. Both you white boys is crazy, and I ain't crazy." "Then take the gun," I say. He reaches for it. "Great, now we're all screwed," Pat says, throwing his arms up and walking out of the cafeteria. "Wait," I say, "we have to talk about what we're up against.

Obviously everyone knows about zombies, but I think a refresher course might do us some good." Pat laughs out loud. "Zombies! Not real my friend." "Go outside and tell me they're not real," I say, but he ignores me. "If anyone wants to go about this in a rational way, follow me," Pat says, and heads for the men's locker room to the left of the three basketball courts. Zombies might not be real, but whatever's outside is.

When Pat left, Ryan Peterson and the old man in his tattered basketball jersey went with him. That left me, Abby, George, Kevin, and Miss Seton in the cafeteria. We have one gun. I'm not even sure what the hell it is, I just know that it does the trick as long as you hit the bastards in the head. And outside, there's a lot of bastards. "It's a Glock 22," George says. He must've seen me eyeing it in his hand. "I've been at the wrong end of this bad boy too many times to count," he says. No one meets his eyes except me. So I just nod. "I don't care what it is as long as it keeps me alive enough to get to my fiancé." "How many times you shoot it?" he asks. "I counted three." I shake my head. "I don't know.

Burnett talked about shooting down at the festival." "He could be carrying an extra magazine on him. I'm not about to go in there and find out, though," George says. Good idea, I think. "I don't think it'll matter. Those things get in here, then we're going to need a lot more shots than that." Miss Seton squeaks like a mouse at the table next to the rest of us. I catch Abby's eyes. They're wet and shiny. Kevin looks a little pale, but otherwise, he's his Freaky strong-self, which I'm still having trouble adjusting to. "So headshots," Kevin says. "Zombies and headshots, huh?" My finger comes up to linger in the middle of my forehead, between the eyes. "Right here," I say. "Enough!" Miss Seton says. "I don't want to hear this.

Enough!" The guilt hits me full-force now. She's right. This is nothing to brag about. But I can't help it. Growing up killing all kinds of crazy creatures in video games, seeing people shoot people on TV and in movies like nothing has taken a toll on my psyche. I'm practically living my wildest dreams. The Death Slayer may not have been well-received by critics, but it has a soft spot in my heart. "These are people you're talking about," Miss Seton continues. "Tony was the kindest man I knew.

He gave me a job when no one else would. I went nearly thirty years as a homemaker. I raised my kids, practically raised a grandkid, too. Being a wife and a mom and a grandmother was all I knew." Her old lady perfume hits my nostrils hard enough to give me a headache, it reminds me of my mom, and if it smelt a little better, it would remind me of Diane. "I was in my fifties. Never touched a computer in my life. Didn't own a cell phone. No discernible skills whatsoever. All I had with me was the grace of God in my heart and hope in my pocket. Steve died of a heart attack. My kids are gone, off doing their own thing, and here I am, alone and afraid.

It's like I'm sixteen again only this time with bad knees. Tony hired me on the spot. He's been nothing but nice and pleasant to me. A man like him doesn't deserve to die the way he did. To be mutilated. And Becky, don't even get me started on Becky, she went to school with my oldest daughter. She was a star athlete. A gentle person." Her eyes blaze with fire, except the back of my mind tells me that it's not fire, but it's actually the wrath of God. I don't speak. Can't speak. "Mr. Huber is right. This is a fantasy. It has to be," Miss Seton moans. "Hold on. Who's Mr. Huber?" I ask. "Pat," Miss Seton says. "Son of a bitch," I say under my breath.

Now I know why that asshole looks familiar. He's Freddy Huber's father. My hand absentmindedly goes up to the bandage under my eye. Leave it to me to get trapped in a place with my high school bully's equally asshole of a father. "If you think Pat's right, Fiona, then go right ahead and join him," Abby says, bringing me back to earth. "You know where he went. This place isn't that big." She narrows her eyes at the old woman, who seems to tower over all of us.

If she holds her chin any higher, I'm afraid her head might roll down her back. "Perhaps I will," she says. "Just remember, lady, we have the gun," George says. He tilts it in his hand so some of the dim lighting flashes off of the barrel. "And you remember, sir, I have God. There's no better defense than His grace," she says and turns to walk away. That awful perfume goes with her, and I say a silent prayer of thanks. "Get it together, y'all," George snaps. "We got bigger fish to fry than what those people are on." "He's right," Kevin says. "What do we do?" Abby asks.

That gleam of tears is back in her eyes. "Not too many options," I say. "We can wait it out, hope the Army shows up and blows them all to hell. Or we make an escape. Those doors won't hold forever." "You think the Army will show?" Kevin asks, his eyebrows moving closer together on his spray-tanned face. I think of my brother and how selfish he was growing up, how selfish he probably still is. He's Army, and really, I wouldn't want my fate in his hands. If he's been eaten by now, let's just say I wouldn't be devastated. "Nah, man, they ain't coming. Think of where we are at right now," George says. Nobody talks. "We are in the middle of nowhere. Prestonpans, Scotland isn't England.

All the people here are old, retired white folk or trailer trash. They're gonna be gone within the next decade." "So?" I say. "That means we ain't top priority. England is a big, big place if you ain't noticed. They'll try to save the cities first. Their precious Fortune 500 companies, big-wigs in their air conditioned, million-pound offices. A small country town like Prestonpans is shit on the bottom of their boots. The thought depresses me because it's true. "Besides, all I saw is one person go crazy and rip someone to shreds. Just one person," George says. "The rest are just banging against the doors like dummies. "Yeah, but there's tons of them out there," I say.

Maybe if there was one or two, we'd be okay. "They were still coming before we got in and locked the emergency exit," Abby says. "One attacked me!" Kevin says defensively. "Don't you hear them?" I ask. "No, I don't hear them. And now I don't see them because this whole place is made of brick and there's like one damn window, not to mention you made us block the front doors." "Be my guest, George, go look." "Whoa, cool it, Carly. I'm just sayin' if they were all like that cop was then why wouldn't they be inside by now?" "Dead people aren't properly adept at using a door handle," I say. "Go look, George.

You've got the gun. Go take a peek outside." I'm challenging him. He seems like the kind of fellow who'll eat up any challenge. Besides, I want to confirm my sanity. If I'm going to lead this group to safety and in turn lead myself to Diane, I need them all behind me. He cocks the gun back, looks me dead in the eyes. "Where's the nearest exit, Abby?" he asks. She shakes her head. "You can't be serious? I saw what's out there. You don't want to, believe me." "Nearest exit, Abby, or I'm going through the front doors." She sighs, knowing he'll find it himself if she doesn't answer. "Around the corner, past the first basketball court." George turns to leave.

# Chapter Twelve

George's sneakers squeak on the honey-colored basketball court. He moves at a jog until he comes up on the white curtain between the track and courts. It parts, chains jingling, knocking some dust bunnies free. Set in the brick wall, a square window of thick, frosted glass distorts the images outside. I see a picture-perfect sunset. Orange, and purplish pink. Cotton candy skies. There's a building on this side of the gym adjacent to the massive parking lot dotted with cars. It's a church, and part of me wants to yell out to Miss Seton so she can get her religious ass over there, but I don't think yelling is a good idea at this point.

I don't see any more zombies outside. The Recreation center is pretty big, and the crowd seemed dense by the front and side doors. Maybe there's a chance over here. Maybe we can get out. Maybe I can get to Diane before they get to her. Will she still love me knowing I'm a murderer? I don't know. But I'm willing to find out. Above the door, in bright-red letters reads:

EMERGENCY EXIT ALARM WILL SOUND IF DOOR IS OPENED.

"George, wait up," I say. I need to stop this before it gets out of hand. He pauses, wheels around to face me with the gun lowered. I flinch, seeing the dark steel. "Now what?" he asks. "I don't think it's a good idea to open the door. The alarm is gonna sound. That'll just bring them over here if they're not over here already." "The electricity is off, dummy. Did it go off when you and the chick went out the other one?" "No, it didn't..." I say, but that one looked ancient in comparison to the one we stand at now.

"What about the backup generators...dummy?" Kevin says. "Those generators concentrate on what's important," George says. "Lights, refrigeration systems, air conditioning. The alarm ain't going to sound." He pauses at the window, cups his hands around his face, gun still in the right one. "Looks like a beautiful day to me." I hang back a few feet.

I'm on the rubber track. It's dark over here, no emergency lights like the ones in the cafeteria and the front desk area. "Seriously, man, it's not a good idea," I say. "I was just joking. You don't have to prove your manliness or anything like that. Let's go back to the cafeteria and come up with a plan." Kevin is even farther behind me. Abby's on my hip, she digs in her pocket for the key and tosses it to George. I look at her sideways. "Really?" "I want to get out of here, too," she says. "And he has the gun."

I can't argue with that. George leans up against the cross handle, sticks the key in the hole, and unlocks the bar with a snap. With his free hand, he swipes it over the stubbled hair atop his head. I see his knuckles flash white through his skin as he grips the gun. "Here goes nothing," he says. His sneaker catches the track with a squeal as he backs into the door. It opens. So far, no alarm. No zombies, either. I'm struck by how quiet it is outside. No sounds at all except for nature. Birds tweeting. Wind rustling leaves high in the trees. George's ragged breath. More importantly, no death rattles from the freaks.

It's a peaceful, almost eerie moment. I try to take it in. There's not been a time in my life I can remember where I'm fully conscious and I don't hear the sounds of cars rolling down the road, the horns honking, people arguing. There's never been this much silence. I take a half-step across the threshold. I'm scared, I'll admit it, but I'm also intrigued. Did I see what I saw in the lobby? Did Tony really get ripped apart by a zombie cop, and did I shoot one of them by the dumpster? I think I did. Or is it just my writer's imagination out of control? Diane. I think of Diane. There's no time to second guess what I saw or didn't see.

I have to get to her, even if this is all some fucked up hallucination. Right now, that's what it seems like. Just, my imagination in overdrive, coping with the death of my mother, Freddy Huber's punch, and the re-appearance of my brother. Then I hear it. Then I see it. My brain doesn't fully comprehend what happens at first. It's too busy trying to soak up this still, and possibly, dying world. A faint red light dances above the frame. I'm about three feet out of the opening. Kevin goes pale. Abby plugs her ears. All the lights flick on in the recreation center. A scoreboard buzzer goes off, signifying the end of a game no one was playing on one of the courts.

The red flashes speed up, and the alarm sounds just like the sign warned us it would. The power has come back on for the time being. The worst possible time too. George looks a little frazzled from the alarm, but he turns to me and shrugs. "Ain't nothin out here. I'm going home." "But they're drawn by sound," I say, thinking of Carly Death slayer's radio alarm going off as a herd of zombies passed outside the house he takes refuge in, thinking of how all the zombies turned at the same time and broke down his door. But I made that up like I could be making this up.

I don't know. I just don't know. "Fire department will be here soon, kid. I wish you the best." Behind me, Kevin and Abby are scrambling to turn the alarm off. The door was new, but the alarm wasn't. All it is is a giant bell perched up above the frame with a small hammer ding-dinging at a million miles per hour. George spreads his arms like a man who'd been locked away in a prison for thirty years as opposed to a man trapped in a gym for less than two hours. He closes his eyes, inhales deeply. The wind blows, billowing the edges of his loose-fitting shirt.

In the trees, it looks like a great monster shakes awake from its slumber, disturbed by the emergency exit alarm. But there's no monster. Only a flock of birds that fly from the branches. "Get that alarm off!" Pat shouts. Him and his little group of invalids follow him from their campsite on the last basketball court, probably discussing ways on how to assassinate me. Wow, I am going crazy. First, I think it's a prank, and now I think I'm important enough to be assassinated.

Kevin jumps as I turn my head. When he lands on the rubber track, the whole ground seems to shake. The alarm continues; it's definitely real. "Seriously, shut that thing off!" Pat says again. Miss Seton puts a hand over her mouth, tilts her head up at Pat. He's sweaty again. "It's driving me crazy!" Pat says. "I'm trying!" Kevin's deep voice rumbles over the sound of the dings. He jumps, and I hear a loud thwack and him sucking in breath through his teeth. Because it's silent. The big bastard actually punched the bell until it shut up. No one says anything for a moment.

Pat wears that same conniving smile that never seems to leave his face. "Where are your precious zombies, Glass?" he asks, squaring up like he might hit me. "Leave the kid alone, man," George says. "He bull-shitted us. They all did. The little whore who works here, and that big buffoon," Pat says as if he never saw Tony get ripped apart, as if he thinks this is all one, big practical joke. But did he? Did I? Is this bullshit? Pat gives George a death stare, then he grabs me by the collar. "Give me the gun! I'm gonna teach this pipsqueak who to bullshit." George stands there with it in hand.

I see him out of the corner of my eye, like he's actually contemplating letting this dick-head put a bullet in my brain. There's no way he is. Just no way. "I told you motherfuckers he is crazy. You know what, let's just forget all of this, go back to our cars, back to our families, and get on with our lives," George says. "What do you say?" Pat's face goes a shade whiter. Maybe he's not as crazy as he looks. Even if he lets go of me, I'm punching him in the face the first chance I get, zombies or not.

Then there's that sound. At first, I think it comes from the back of Pat's throat, but the sound echoes, doubles, triples. They aren't human sounds. They aren't sounds that come from someone that's alive. They're the gurgles of the dead ringing in my ear the same way they rang in my head when I wrote about them. Limbs wrap around the bricks, arms and legs searching aimlessly. Then a face. It's a face of someone slightly recognizable like maybe I saw him at the grocery store, maybe he was a suggested friend on Facebook. I just don't remember his profile picture having so much blood in it.

The lights sputter. Flicker. They go off. Pat lets go of my collar, his jaw dropping open. "Aw, shit, man," George says. Behind me, Abby screams. "Get in," I say. George is about twenty feet from the door, but the dead cut off his escape route back into the building. "Move!" Pat says, then shoulders me out of the way. I go barreling into the door frame pretty hard. It hurts, but I'm in shock so I hardly notice. It'll hurt worse later. Pat reaches for the handle. "No!" I yell. "There's no time," he says. He might be right. George raises the gun toward the crowd. It's thick with distorted faces, shiny blood, and crooked limbs. Each zombie has a sickening, ashy quality to them.

They look like that because they're dead. Because, this is real. Because, I'm not going crazy. The gun goes off, and the leader of the crowd goes down in a spray of blood and pallid skin. Pat pulls the door closed. I'm reliving Tony all over again. How I tried to save him. How I failed. I don't want it to be like that, so I ram my own shoulder through the crack, wedge myself between safety and death. I have no weapons, no plan, and the forest of zombies grows thicker by the second. They're attracted to the sounds. With Abby and Miss Seton's screaming, it's a wonder the whole dead world hasn't shown up yet. "Come on, George!" I say.

He still aims the weapon toward the crowd to my right, but on my left, there's even more. The only place uncovered with them is the church across from us. If we run there are too many fences to climb, barriers to get past, and how long until more of them show up? Zombies shamble down the pavement, dragging broken legs and feet, moaning, mouths shining with red. George catches my eyes. "So be it, kid," Pat says. "I'm closing the door." It's funny, really. I was the one who tried to convince Pat, and now he's going to live and I'm going to die.

I'm going to get eaten by the townspeople of Prestonpans. What a way to go. Make sure they have a closed coffin at my funeral, just like Mother! "No, he's not," Kevin's voice booms. "Hey, asshole," Pat says. I hear the dull thud of Kevin's massive mitts hitting the steel door. "Come on," Kevin says. George turns to run, the crowd right on his heels. A straggler reaches out, barely snags the loose hem of his sweatpants as she falls to the asphalt. She's a fat woman, and even in death, her face looks hungry. It's not enough to bring George down with her, but it's enough to trip him up.

He stumbles, and the gun goes sprawling off the pavement, sliding toward the encroaching crowd to my left. Fear seizes my throat. We'll need that gun, even if we're out numbered, we'll need it. As I reach out and grab it, a vomit-smelling dead man lunges at me. It's as if when the zombies see potential meals, they speed up, not an attribute in my zombie fiction, even I'm not that sadistic. I grab the weapon, and George grabs me as I stumble forward. Something falls from my pocket, and I feel my heart break when I realize it's the keys to my rental car. They skitter across the asphalt like it's ice, now lost in a sea of dead flip-flops.

Kevin yanks us both before I can even think of trying to get them back, then pulls us through while pulling the door shut with his free hand. "Oh, my God. Oh, my God," Abby says. She jingles her keychain, fumbles with the right one, then finally sticks it into the lock and clicks it closed. This changes my plans of escape. The motel isn't that far from the recreation center, but I damn sure wasn't planning on walking. I will have to if it's the only way. To save the girl of my dreams, I would do anything. Just hold on a little longer. Please, God, let Diane hold on a little longer. "What the hell is wrong with you?" I say to George.

He's sweating, breathing hard, chest rising and falling in a stuttered pattern. "I-I don't know, It seemed safe. They weren't there, then they were. What the fuck are they? Are those really...zombies?" "Yes," I say with one hundred percent surety. I turn to Pat. I want to be pissed at the guy, but if I were in his position, I would've done the same, so instead of going off on him, I just say, "Now do you believe me?" He shrugs. "Something's up, sure, but zombies? C'mon, Glass, that's just bullshit and we all know it."

His face tells me something different. He's in denial. Rightfully so. "No such thing as the dead coming back to life, no matter how many times you write about it in your stupid, fucking books." "They were dead, man," George says. "I looked them right in the eyes. Just blank. Dead, man. Fuckin dead." Pat snorts. "This ain't funny, dude. We almost lost the gun. And there's about a million of those things out there. They ain't playing around, either," George says. We all stare at each other. There's an odd silence for a moment until it's ruined by the sounds of thumping fists and gurgling moans. I see their shadows pass under the door. They thunder against the metal. It sounds like a storm.

I start to back away, the rest of the group following me. We get to the basketball court entrance before we split up again. "Crazy," Pat says before he turns down the dark hallway. I walk across the cafeteria. Everyone stops there. Chairs scoot across the tile. But I keep walking. There's an indoor soccer field adjacent to the cafeteria made of turf. I walk to the door and open it. The ground is soft, almost like real grass. I slide down the safety wall and onto the field, then take my shoes off. "I need to get out of here," I say to myself. Diane is a strong woman, but she wouldn't know what to do to a zombie if the things could talk and tell her. She'll be scared, frightened, help-less.

Those things outside, call them zombies or not, are deadly, and I need to get to her, need to protect her before it's too late. And I know it's not too late. Diane and I have this connection. I don't want to sound cliché or too lovey-dovey (like one of her vomit-inducing romance books), but we don't have two hearts, we only have one. We are connected at this spiritual level. If she died, I believe I would feel it. Instead, I just feel anxiety and worry from both of us. She is still okay. She has to be. Please, God, if you let me get out of here alive, and you let Diane be okay, I promise I'll start going to church. I'll stop saying swear words. I'll stop eating red meat and watching porn.

There's hardly any light above me. Just one, emergency backup that casts shadows. I don't know what I was expecting. A harp, maybe an

angel coming down from the heavens to assure me it'll be okay. Instead
of clouds, this place smells like a locker room. Like sweaty gym socks. I
really, really need to get out of here. I get an idea. Nobody gets anything
done by sitting around and sulking. I shoot up and head out of the
soccer field. Abby and Kevin are sitting at their table. She has her head
down, while Kevin is messing with his phone. The screen is lit up, and
he's swiping something.

A flutter of hope freezes my heartbeat. Maybe he's getting service.
"Working?" I ask. "No," he says. "Piece of shit cell phone." Behind me,
something rattles. "Damn it," George says. He holds the Coca-Cola
vending machine by each side and rocks it back and forth. "After the
shit I went through I think I deserve a drink. But no, the backup
generator ain't gonna send no power to the vending machines, is it? Just
my luck." "Break it," Abby says. He raises his eyebrows. "What?" "Yeah,
just break it. The manager isn't going to yell at you. The Officer is dying,
or already dead. You won't get in trouble." "Girl's right," Kevin says, not
looking up from his phone. "I think your crime will be forgiven under
our circumstances." "You're right." He grabs a chair, picks it up, and uses
the legs to shatter the glass. One hit was all it took. He grabs a Coke
in one hand, and a couple more in the other. "Anyone want one?" I
raise my hand, and he tosses me one. Kevin shakes his head. "End of the
world or not, carbs are carbs."

We all laugh, but it's not a laugh you'd expect from a group of
friends all having a good time. It's a shaky laugh, one I think we let out
to help keep our sanity. Abby takes a bottle of water. "We get saved and
someone asks who broke the machine, y'all gonna have my back when
I blame Pat?" More of that uneasy laughter. "That cop got any other
weapons?" George asks. "Just a nightstick," Abby answers. "Shit, is that
him right there?" George says. George sits across from me. I'm facing
the broken vending machine.

He faces the front doors. My mind says no that can't be him. I
locked the door. "Look," George says again, holding up the hand that

has the Coke in it. I turn around. The front desk is almost completely shrouded in darkness. Only a sliver of daylight peeks over the trees across the recreation center and comes in through the small window. There's a silhouette standing at the desk. It's impossible to tell who the person is, but I see the utility belt around the shadow's waist. The head is crooked, leaning away to the right, and there's a lump on its neck. Like a towel, I'm thinking. Something about his eyes, too. They glow faintly. "No, God, please, no," I say.

Kevin looks away from his phone. I explode up. This is my fault. I should've done what needed to be done in that room. I had the gun. I had a broken broom handle. He practically begged me to do it. But I couldn't. "He's turned," I say, my voice more shaky than I intend it to be. "I was going to put him down, but I wasn't sure if he'd turn. I needed to be a hundred percent sure. And I thought the door was locked..." I'm babbling again. Abby, George, and Kevin freeze next to me.

I was right. I didn't want to be, but I was right all along. "You mean he's one of them," Abby says. She speaks like she doesn't want to believe it, like she's oblivious to the rules of zombies. Her tone is almost like Pat's was. "Stay back," I say to them, filling my hand with the gun. I'm going to do what I should've done the first time.

# Chapter Thirteen

As I get closer, I have to make sure he's really turned before I put a bullet through his brain. It's too dark, so I move until I'm able to tell. By this time, Officer Burnett lunges at me, and I'm not quick enough. A pair of gnarled hands grip me around the collar. We topple over the front desk, hearing the unmistakable sound of the gun clattering off the tile and being swallowed up by the darkness.

I can't even scream because his dead weight lands on my stomach, driving all the breath from my lungs. George jumps in and grabs the Officer by his shoulders, pushing him away from me. The air fills my lungs quick. I take a deep breath before trying to claw myself away in the opposite direction. Burnett is on his hands and knees. The towel fell off during our little trip over the desk, and now the bite mark shows. It's black and blue and red. I see some foam around the edges. The sight is bad, but the smell is worse, even worse than it was in the athletic room.

I see Abby and Kevin stop then start backing up out of my peripherals as we watch this zombified version of Burnett crawl toward us. George isn't scared, at least I think he's not. He's breathing heavy and fast, staring at the Officer on his hands and knees with a look of pure hatred. Burnett lunges again, except this time I'm prepared for it. George slides out of the way, throws a punch into the back of the dead guy's head. It doesn't do much but speed him toward me. I raise my leg up, not to kick, but to keep him away.

It's enough to send him into the glass partition separating the entrance and exit. "Quick, give me something to bust his head!" George shouts. The front of the recreation hall is pretty bare. Everything that had weight to it is pressed up against the doors in a heap of junk. I scan the pile real quick, see a set of twenty-five pound weight plates stacked up against the legs of the waiting area couch. Burnett is in between me and the pile, and George is too busy. He won't even take his eyes off the thing. I don't blame him, not since what happened outside. One false move and you could be on the pavement getting devoured.

We saw it first-hand. Burnett grapples at me, but I dodge it easily. He gets nothing besides air, moaning as he does it. When I pass him, the smell of his rotting flesh is almost enough to make me pass out right then and there, but I don't. I grab the twenty-five pounder. It's heavier than I'd think twenty-five pounds was, but then again, I'm kind of a weakling. "Here," I say. George takes it, raises the plate above his head. His arms bulge with muscles. Veins dance. He brings it down on Burnett's face. It's not a clean hit. Instead, the metal scrapes the side of the face. Skin peels off of him like those string cheeses Mother used to pack in my lunchbox everyday in fourth grade, except a lot more moldy and gross.

Twenty-five pounds sounds like a thunderbolt when it hits the tiles, then it sounds even louder when it rolls into the glass partition, taking a chunk out with it. Outside the moans get louder. Kevin keeps shuffling away with Abby behind him. George is frozen, and so am I. If we had the gun, this could be over. "Kevin! Look for the gun!" I shout. "It fell somewhere behind the desk." "I'm not getting near that thing," he says, and I'm assuming he means Burnett, who stands by the desk.

Then Burnett advances on us with only half a face. I can see the cheekbone, part of his nose cartilage all glazed over with a bloody thick sheet. He's basically mutilated, yet he keeps coming. "You gotta hit him harder than that," I say over Burnett's death rattles. "Be my guest, buddy," George says to me over his shoulder. "Seriously, a weight plate? You couldn't find anything more practical than that?" I pick up another twenty-five pounder, this time I don't pass it off to George. This is my moment. This is where I save the day, all my deepest and darkest fantasies are going to be lived out.

I am Carly Death Slayer, I'll have to be if I want to get to Diane. What will happen when the gun runs out of bullets? What will happen when the only weapon I have handy is some blunt object? I'll have to smash some brains in, that's what. Burnett advances. "Do something, you big oaf!" Abby says, I'm assuming to Kevin. I throw the weight at Burnett's feet. Nothing, I barely got it there. I am not Carly Death Slayer. A chunk of tile shatters. Dust wafts into the air. A small chair is wedged under the couch. I pry it free and point it legs first at Burnett. Some of the barricade falls behind me. The moaning seems to increase. Burnett hits the legs, but they don't slow him down. In fact, he's stronger than I initially thought he'd be. He drives me into the brick wall near the doors. Something circular and metal digs into my back.

I hear a beep-beep, then the sounds of motors whirring. The door next to me clicks over and over as it cracks open about half a foot, then closes, blocked by most of the stuff we stacked up here and the tied jump ropes. God forbid a handicapped person can't open the doors when the power goes out. Really, it was only a matter of time. If one of us didn't hit the button in here, then one of them would've out there. If we would've kept quiet long enough for the Army to show up, we might've survived. Oh, well. Shuffling feet scrape across the lobby carpet. The death rattles fill the air.

A hand pops through the crack in the doors, then a face with its flesh melting off the bone. Teeth snap like an angry dog. Thanks, backup generator. Really, thanks a lot. Burnett's hands swipe at my head. A finger brushes my cheek. I know a scratch will do it, too. I'm lucky he just tickles me. "Shit," George says. He picks up another plate, raises it. A whistle sounds above. "Hey, ugly!" Pat yells from upstairs. I look up to see his face shrouded in darkness. He holds something silver and bulky in his hand. "Not you, Glass. I'm talking to your friend."

Burnett's neck creaks as he looks up, fresh blood spills from the wound. Pat smiles. I see the flash of his eyes, the gleam of his white teeth. Then the gleam of the dumbbell as it comes careening over the side. It all happens so fast: the splat, the spray of scarlet and bones, and the lack of force pressed up against me. Burnett drops harder than the dumbbell. I see the 75 etched into each end of it, covered in sticky blood. I'm covered, too.

Droplets roll off of my face, down my nose and onto the mess on the floor. "Thanks," I say to Pat, shaking my head. I never thought I'd willingly thank a Huber in my life. "Yo, that's nasty," George says. I glance over my shoulder. The teeth are still snapping in my direction through the crack in the door triggered by the handicap assistance button. "We have to barricade the doors again," I say. George throws his shoulder into the couch, trying to drive the thing back into the lobby. I hear more moans, more death rattles. The group from the outside is now inside the lobby. I risk a peek and see about fifty bodies all stumbling and bumbling about. It's definitely a fire hazard because the sign on the wall, in the background above this snapping freak's head says the lobby can only house thirty people.

George grunts as the couch starts to slide forward. Knuckles and elbows and hands beat on the glass. Soon it won't hold, no matter how many couches and jump ropes we use. I slide over, careful not to slip in the goo and brains from the thing that used to be Burnett and start pushing my hands up against the couch. A sweat breaks out on my forehead. I'm grunting, trying to will myself to get stronger, but it's no use. The knocking grows rapid. To my left, I hear glass break. They're almost in, and we're almost screwed.

The group just stands there. "Any help would be nice," George says, grunts, actually. Nobody moves until Pat moves. When Miss Seton raises a finger, points to the wall at the mess that was once Burnett, she screams. It seems to motivate the zombies. They push with a force that George and I can't match. We almost fall. "We have to fight!" I say to George. He just shakes his head, already knowing it to be true. "Ain't got much to fight with." "Freddy, we have to fight," I say to them. "Grab a weapon." "No way," Ryan, the janitor says.

"Those doors open, and I'm gone, I'm running all the way up to North Berwick to check on my mom and dog." I grit my teeth as a weight plate drives into the heel of my shoe. "Be my guest," I say. "But good luck, because if this many are attacking us, think of how many are out there just waiting for a snack. The festival brings in like twenty-thousand people. Do you like your chances out there on your own? At least wait until we can group up and fight our way out together." Ryan's face goes a little pale at that. He knows I'm right. "We fight," Pat agrees, and again I never thought a Huber would agree with me. He holds a barbell in one hand. It's a shorter one, mainly used for working out your biceps. It has grooves in the middle for your hands. Not too heavy. Not too light. A genius idea. "Everyone go get a weapon," he says, then looks at Miss Seton with her head in her lap as if she's going to be sick. "Yes, you, too, Fiona." "We can't hold it much longer, man," George says. "Everyone go get weapons!" Pat's voice booms.

They rush up the steps. A few moments later, they're back. Kevin holds a barbell, one of the big ones used for benching and squatting. I think they weigh close to fifty pounds, and he holds it like it weighs five. Abby has a kettle bell in each hand. They don't look heavy, but they look hard enough to smash a skull. The old basketball player has a couple of the colored dumbbells that virtually weigh next to nothing. Ryan has a broomstick, go figure, but the end looks sharpened to a very fine point.

Kind of surprising and also kind of alarming. Like how long has this creep been sharpening a broom stick, and for what unholy reason? Miss Seton slinks back behind the rest of them, empty-handed. "Ready?" I shout as if we have a choice. "We let go, then you and I get armed, and we defend this gym." I know the gun is somewhere nearby and my fingers itch to use it, but I also know it would be a bad idea. I'm inexperienced and untrained.

An XBOX controller is not a gun, I'm old enough to know that. Besides, together we can hold this group off without bullets. "Ready," George says. I spring forward away from the doors, George follows.

I'm about five steps away before I turn around and look at the carnage. Arms and legs and faces poke through the fractured glass. The doors swell as if they are about ready to explode. The rattles from deep in the back of their throats get louder. "Cover us!" I run up the steps, not looking over my shoulder, too afraid to look over my shoulder.

The weight room looks like it's been ransacked. Plates and bars are on the floor, scattered. A couple of benches are overturned. A treadmill belt looks to be off its track. The ellipticals are stacked against each other like fallen dominoes. I find one of those twisted barbells with the grooves for your hands. George picks up a set of dumbbells, scooting them over to the edge of the guardrail, ready to drop them on the crowd when they break in. Me, well, I run back down the stairs, of course. I don't want to, but I have to. Even if we all die, I don't want to die afraid. I don't want to die knowing that everyone here knew I was afraid. I want them to see me fight until the end. I want to die fighting my way to Diane, and I'm ready to die for her.

I just hope she knows this. People scream, and I'm not sure exactly who it is. It's like a conglomeration of all the survivors' screams. "They're coming!" Pat says. "Stay calm!" Glass shatters. Something that sounds like the couch toppling over and rolling a few feet follows. Then comes the moans, the rattles, all amplified tenfold. "Heads up!" George says. He throws over a fifty-pound dumbbell. A fat woman with a Nike, visor take the brunt of the weight on the side of her head and left shoulder. She falls to the floor like a heap of bricks.

The rest of the dead walk over her as if nothing happened. Next goes a thirty-five pounder which misses badly. They keep coming. George now comes down the stairs with two of the curled barbells in hand. Kevin grunts as he swings his barbell into the face of about five of those things. The blur of metal is nauseating to look at, and the spray of blood even more so. Pat is near the front desk, and he's raising his bar like a wizard raises a staff, bringing it down on the soft skull of the woman who'd been hit with the fifty-pound dumbbell.

My heart lifts a little when I see the doors. Out of the six, only two are breached beyond repair. The glass is gone and most of the barricade is scattered about, but we can barricade it again. Another good thing about this is that it constricts the flow of zombies to only two doors. Against the backdrop of the waning, yellow sun, I see there's a lot more than I expected, but if the other doors hold and we continue to fight, we can hold out for a little while.

My first swing is a large miss. I aim for the head and wind up hitting the hard torso of a guy about my age. He has a smeared American flag painted on his face. Blood runs from his eyes, and his features don't change when the metal connects with his chest. The hit was hard enough to crack the sternum, and as a matter of fact, I do hear a crack, but it's as if I never touched him. He keeps coming. Behind him, three more are walking in my direction. I cock the barbell back again, this time like a man throwing a javelin instead of a baseball player swinging a bat. The end of the dumbbell is round, but it's still metal. And I crack Face-Paint square in the forehead. His skull splits open. Pink goo oozes from the wound, and he stumbles around like a drunk, before falling over. Wow, I really did it, and I'm laughing. I'm officially in one of my own damn books.

How surreal. How freaking surreal. I don't know whether to laugh, cry, or scream. Abby rushes past me. "Look out," she says, both kettle bells in hand. She pirouettes over the crumpled body of Face-Paint. A rush of wind slaps me in the face, followed by a smell of sweat and death. The kettle bells come together. It's a dead man sandwich on iron bread. The old dude who was about three steps from tearing my throat out doesn't have a face anymore. A spurt of blood flies at me, one that I barely dodge. Then the old zombie crumples to the floor.

More bodies walk over him, their tennis shoes and flip-flopped feet stomp out the rest of his brains. A guy in a cowboy hat Frankensteins toward me, you know, arms out, mouth hanging open, dead noises coming from the back of his throat, and I swing the barbell up with a metal uppercut. His teeth turn to powder, and he's lifted off his feet. It's not bloody or messy, but it's enough. He falls next to his old friend, unmoving. More glass shatters.

The ones who can't fit in through the broken entrance doors now try to squeeze in through the barrier we made against the four exit doors. I rush over there, giving Abby a nod. She nods back, spins, and cracks a woman in a bloody tank top. Kevin grunts; it echoes high in the rafters. He swings the barbell like a great knight wielding a sword. Metal clashes against tile and wood, and most importantly, skulls.

# Chapter Fourteen

A rotten smell is in the air, and at that moment I long for Diane's cherry-scented shampoo. Hell, I'd even take her morning breath over the graveyard of piling bodies in the lobby. "Push them toward the doors," Abby says somewhere away from me. George runs over to me. He has the gun, now. "I'm gonna shoot them!" he yells. "No bullets," I say. We've come this far without them, we can keep going. A face pokes through the shattered window. Black spit oozes from the corners of their mouth. It is a man, maybe age thirty, but it could also be a woman with short hair. At this point, I'm not sure because they all look like each other.

They all look dead. George nods, then he flips the gun around and starts hammering that gross face with the butt of the gun. A squishy, squelching sound follows. "Now you got the idea," I say, raising the barbell, poking it through the crack. It's like playing a horrid game of pool and the heads who stick their hungry, emaciated faces near the window are the cue balls.

Blood sprays here, blood sprays there, and the bodies fall. Still, the doors swell as the bulk of the towns-people press against the frames and the couches. I glance over my shoulder at the carnage behind us. Lots of bodies lie in pools of blood and sprinkled brains. It looks like a battlefield. Fiona stands on the steps, no weapon in hand, like a woman on a chair trying to avoid a mouse in the house. Her face is as white as a piece of paper. For a moment, I feel bad for her.

Kevin brings the barbell up high enough to almost knock the dead lights hanging above us. Something like a foot stuck in mud fills my ears. I can't see who he hits, but I see the spray of blood against the glass divider, hear him cry out in horror. Zombie killing is a messy business. "Help us!" I shout. This time, they all come over. Abby swipes the back of her arm across her forehead, smearing red. Kevin jogs. Pat, the old man, and Ryan don't rush.

I throw my back against the lower end of the couch to stay away from the hands that stick through the broken window, then wedge my feet against a couple of bodies in front of me. "Not gonna hold," Pat says. He wipes away the gunk off the end of his barbell, stepping on dead limbs and faces, not even caring about his tennis shoes. "It will if we all help," I say. "Yeah, asshole," Abby says. I can't help but smile.

I wonder how long she's been waiting for the right time to say that. Working here, she probably has to put up with his bullshit constantly. I give her an approving nod. She could be like the little sister I never had. "This is unholy," the old man says. "In all my years, I've never seen anything like this." His eyes take up most of his wrinkled face. He could be in his sixties or possibly his nineties, there's no middle ground. "We got this," I say, waving him away. It's hard to talk while pushing backward, but I manage it. "You sure son?" "Yeah, just get up there with Miss Seton. Keep her company. Don't worry, we'll get this under control," I say.

I think he's more use to us up there than down here, but I don't say it aloud. To my left, Pat snorts and says, "Yeah, right," under his breath. Ryan chuckles nodding.

Luckily, the old man is too old to hear it, or maybe he just chooses not to. I don't know. "There," Kevin says. I turn to look at him. He's wedged the huge barbell diagonally under the frame, blocking the doors from opening. Then he runs off. "Hold it just a little bit longer," he says. In about thirty seconds he's back with three more in hand as if they weigh as much as toothpicks, and he wedges another under the brick arch to make an X, then takes his huge Nikes and kicks them until brick dust rains upon us. It'll hold for the moment it seems, but we really need a plan.

He does the X on the other set of doors, scooting the couches forward while George drops any of the zombies who put their faces near the broken glass with a pair of scissors he must've grabbed from the front counter. "Good idea, Kevin," the old man says. "I guess I'm not as dumb as you say I am, huh, Earl?" Earl snickers. "All right. Now," Kevin says, kicking the barbells until his face is beat red and his gelled hair is frazzled. We move away from the door. For a moment, there are no sounds at all besides the moaning of the crowd outside.

Too good to be true, the doors clang off the bars. Bits of brick powder falls down on the gray iron, coating it in white, but it holds. The glass is broken and the few straggling dead inside the lobby pile up on the barbells quick. Kevin's contraption creaks and groans, but again it holds. George comes forward with the scissors and stabs a few more. The little bit of life the monsters have in their eyes fizzle out.

I think it's all on the tip of our tongues that we know these people. I grew up with some of them. I recognized a teacher. A neighbor. An old friend. How much this hurts, surprises me. But for a moment, it's quiet. We all back away. Earl steps forward, claps Kevin on the back who smiles wide in return. "No, not as dumb as you look, son." Then he says to no one in particular, "Think my wife is gonna be okay?" as he looks out the shattered windows, past the stumbling bodies. "She was making her world famous apple pie for the Bake-Off. I was supposed to see her win the ribbon.

All these years and she's never won. I always say, 'Now, Carol, this year's the year, I promise,' and she never gets discouraged when it's not. I hope she's okay. Please, God..." "Yeah, she is," I say, thinking of my own future wife. "And so is mine. We are going to get out of here, and it's all going to be okay." This time, I mean it because I truly believe it. Pat snorts again. I try to ignore him. "Now let's get out of this mess and get cleaned up," I say to Earl. He nods, and steps toward Miss Seton. Abby looks at me and smiles, "Not a bad first workout, eh?" And right as I start to tell her she's not as funny as she looks, Miss Seton screams.

A gurgle of blood explodes out of the mouth of Cowboy Hat who's supposed to be dead on the floor. Earl falls like a man who's stepped into a bear trap. I can't tear my eyes away from the wave of red that spurts from his leg. It's too late. Cowboy Hat has a gnarled hand around

Earl's ankle. Kevin thunders past me, but he's not fast enough. The zombie on the floor, wearing its dirty clothes and gray skin like some kind of abomination from hell, tears into Earl's chest, right into the exposed skin below his neck.

The white basketball jersey turns a dark red. He flails like a drowning man, one drowning in his own blood. I just stand there, too frozen and shocked to do anything. It's like Tony all over again, except it's not. I'm seasoned now. I've killed these things, I know these things. Kevin's running shoe comes down on the back of Cowboy Hat's head. He cries out like he did when he showed me the correct way to bench press before all this shit went down. Skull crushes beneath sole and tile shatters beneath his face. The head splits open, showing everyone who's willing to look black and pink brains. Cowboy Hat's cowboy hat is now scattered among the rest of the gore.

Tears roll down my face for God knows how long before I muster up the strength to wipe them away. Most of Earl's features are bathed in red. What's not bloody is an ashy pale. His eyes gloss over as his bottom lip trembles. He wheezes and gasps while a bony hand clutches at the wound. Kevin holds his head in his lap while he rocks him back and forth, one of his huge hands tries to quell the bleeding. But it's no use. We all know it. I can see the old man's heart beating through all the gore, and its rhythm slows. A sheen of tears is in the big guy's eyes. I never thought I'd see him cry again. He's no longer the wimp from high school. Men like him don't cry, they just can't. They're too big and burly, too busy slamming back beers and grilling dead cow on world cup day. But then again, I never thought I'd see the dead rise. Never say never, I guess. "L-Look in on Carol," Earl says. "Aw, fuck, man. This shit ain't right," George says.

He drops the barbell he is holding and rubs his hands over his bald pate, turning away. He steps away. I think he might be about to cry, but he damn sure won't do it in front of us. Stupid, I know. He walks past the stairs where Miss Seton looks on through hands that don't quite cover her eyes. Pat has a hand on Ryan's shoulder. He's pinching the bridge of his nose, shaking his head. "Is he gonna be okay?" Abby says next to me, but at this moment it's quiet. Eerily quiet. So quiet that Earl hears her.

And, when he turns his neck, a river of blood flows from between his and Kevin's fingers. "I'm gonna be all right, Abby, yes. I'm going to a better place." His other hand, shakes its way up to the small chain around his neck. Fingers run over the smooth metal of the cross. "It...it was almost my t-time anyway, dear." He laughs. "Please c-check in on Carol f-for me when this is all over. Make sure she got her ribbon. Sometimes she f-forgets to turn off the stove. Her...and t-those soap operas. B-Bet she doesn't even know what's g-goin on. Tell her to start watching t-the news for God's sake. Tell her I-I'm g-gonna be ssss-smiling down on her..." A croak comes from the back of his throat. His eyes open wider. Body shudders, goes stiff. A heel clicks the wet tile and he is gone.

Will he turn now or later? I don't know. In my own books, it takes some time, and even Burnett suffered awhile before he came at us with a craving for human flesh. Earl doesn't, not yet; instead, he just dies right there in front of us all. I hear Abby whimper when she looks to his face where those glossy eyes loom, staring at nothing for the rest of eternity. "Damn, man. What the hell do we do now?" George asks. "We survive," I say.

We have to. I have to...for Diane. "Yeah, in order to do that we gotta get rid of this old fart," Pat says. "You said not to let them bite you. What did he do? He got bit. He's gonna turn now. Zombie 101, right, Carly?" Everyone stares at the man in horror. Sweat isn't soaked through his shirt anymore. It's all dry. Now it's just blood and guts. You can't even tell his shirt was white before all this happened. I'm almost too afraid to look down at myself, at what I look like. As if on cue, all eyes look to me, and the group grimaces.

Then George turns away and says, "Jesus, man, have some respect. Earl was a good guy." "Was," Pat says. "Now he's of no use to us. Don't look at me like this is my fault. Carly is the one who knows so much about these damn things." He laughs, shaking his head. "Zombies." "What do you think we should do?" Abby asks. Kevin is still on the floor, soaked in Earl's blood, tears in his eyes. He rocks back and forth, murmuring slightly. "Well, if the same shit that happened to Burnett happens to Earl " George starts. "Enough," Fiona moans. "Enough. Earl was a kind soul. God would not bestow that fate on him.

The ones out there, those...those things are abominations. They're the souls God rejected for whatever reason, the ones Satan won't even take in. Earl is not one of them." Pat snorts. It's an odd sound in all the quiet chaos. I almost can't breathe let alone snort. "Oh, you knew him, huh, Miss Seton?" Pat says. "Take a look around. Go peer through that broken window and tell me that God is picking and choosing here." Miss Seton steps back like she's been physically slapped. Her mouth hangs open. Eyes drift away from Pat's face. "Then what do we do?" I ask after a moment of awkward silence passes. "Just throw him outside like we're chucking bread to a bunch of ducks?" Pat tilts his head, scratches his chin. "Not a bad idea.

We'll get there, but what I'm saying is if the only way to kill these bastards is to take out the brain, then someone has to bash old Earl's head in." Miss Seton shudders again. "Don't worry, he won't feel it. He's already dead," Pat says. I notice he's smiling like he enjoys this. I think I speak for the rest of us when I say we're one bashed head away from a coronary. "No," Kevin says firmly. "We let him rest." He stands up with the body still in hand. The bleeding has slowed down, but streams dribble from the open wound in his neck like the last vestiges of a rainstorm. Kevin looks bigger and smaller at the same time. He towers over everyone, especially Pat. The two catch eyes and Pat throws his palms up. "Okay, okay, big guy. You'll be the one who buries him then. Better get out there quick before the sun is completely gone." Sundown is soon, I think, but my world has been dark since I lost Diane and this apocalypse happened I hear Kevin's teeth grinding. Somehow, the sound is louder than the snarling in the lobby.

He walks past us toward the steps. I rush toward him, place a hand on his sweaty shoulder. "Here, let me help," I say. When he turns his head to look at me, it's almost in slow motion. Tears and blood clash beneath his eyes, and he falls to one knee, Earl's body still in his arms. "Set him down, man," I say. "Give yourself a rest." I guess even behemoths need to rest sometimes. Kevin listens, rolls Earl's body to the second step. Abby is over now. "You need to go lay down, Kevin. Or eat something."

He chuckles."I'll be all right. Just a little, lightheaded." He sniffles with as much force as a power vacuum. "Come on," Abby says, "we'll go bust open the snack machine. Get you something sugary." "No. No carbs" he says. She grips his arm tight and starts leading him away. When I turn around, Pat's in my face. "You wanna be the leader, kid? Then do something. You know we can't keep him in here. He's a ticking time-bomb. I saw the Officer first-hand." I stammer, trying to think of an answer.

It's amazing how much Pat and Freddy look alike, even more amazing how much I want to punch his lights out. Pat scoffs. "Fuck this." He turns away, bends down to pick something up, then pushes me. It's lightning quick, the movement. A glint of silver flies by my face. He grunts like a warrior as he swings the barbell down onto the second step. Wind whistles by my ear. A couple inches to the left and it could be my head. It's not. It's Earl's head, and his brains and blood spray me like I'm riding the Maid of the Mist through Niagara Falls. "W-Why?" is all I manage to say before Kevin runs over with his fist raised.

My ears are ringing. Words are thrown around, but I don't understand what's going on. All I see is Kevin stop dead in his tracks as Pat raises the pistol in front of him, and aims it at the big guy's head. "Easy there, asshole," Pat says. The ringing stops. I can't blink. Chunks of pink stuff roll down my cheeks and puddle at my feet. There's a fire blazing inside of me. I almost bend down to pick up the barbell, ready to smash Pat's head in, but I think of Diane. If I get myself shot, she's all alone, and I can't be stupid here. Kevin's hands are up. Abby screams, "Stop it! This is too much! Stop...stop...stop!" "You guys want to survive, right?" Pat asks. George reaches in his waistband where the gun should be. "How the hell " "Quick hands," Pat says. "You need to be more careful, buddy. All of us do. And if you guys want to survive then you'll start listening to me. Got it?" "You son of a bitch" George says. Pat levels the gun in his face. "Got it?" he repeats. "Or what?" I say. "Or I'll blow your heads off," Pat says.

That same shit-eating grin is on his face. "Now everyone get where I can see you." He nods his head at me and Miss Seton and Ryan perched on the mid-stair landing to come down and stand in front of him. Then for George to move from his right, and stand next to us. We do. All of our hands are up. Fresh blood and guts line Ryan's work boots. Miss Seton covers her mouth with the heel of her hand. She's relatively clean. There may be a few drops of blood on her red work shirt, but they're basically invisible.

The rest of us...well we look like we've been through hell and back. "As much as I don't want to believe it, as much as I want to believe a few people got high on meth or crack or whatever these dumbasses are smoking these days and decided to chew each other's faces off, that isn't the case. Something is seriously wrong" "You don't say, motherfucker" George starts to say, but is cut off by the sound of Pat cocking the gun. "Respect, my friends, can get you very far in life. Disrespect will get you a bullet in the head. So let's clear things up. I'm in charge.

Whatever I say goes. I don't know how many rounds I got left in this gun, but I'm willing to bet it's enough to put you all down. So what we're going to do is get along, that way I get to keep my hands clean and you guys get to keep your life. Understood?" None of us say anything, but I swivel my head to look at the others. We have hate in our eyes, and

Pat sees it, too because his smile grows wider. He lives and feeds off of it. Somehow, he's worse than his son. Freddy never went homicidal on me. He beat me up and called me names, but he never pointed a gun at my head.

For a moment, the thoughts of Diane are pushed away. REVENGE replaces those thoughts, burning in bright, red letters. Outside, the thudding against the doors grows louder. I look at the mass of hands and fingers prying their way through the makeshift, failing barricade. Those bars aren't going to hold. If God is good they won't and the zombies will pour in and take Pat Huber as their main course. "Pat, please," Miss Seton says. "This isn't you." "Look around, Fiona, this isn't our world. Sometimes, you can't be yourself. Sometimes, you have to change."

# Chapter Fifteen

He herds us upstairs like some kind of macabre sheep. I'm last in line so I get the barrel digging into my back. Pat isn't gentle, either. I feel bad for his wife. He stands guard at the top of the steps, leaning between two water fountains, his eyes flicking from the front doors on the first floor to us as we start building another barricade at the top of the steps. "We wait here until help shows up," Pat says. "No more fighting and killing. We keep our noses out of it until the Army or police get here." "What made you change your mind?" I ask as Ryan and I roll an elliptical machine near the rest of the piled up workout equipment.

Pat narrows his eyes at me. "Don't ask questions, Glass. I want to live. It's that simple. We aren't gonna live out there. We have a better chance in here." Speak for yourself, Pat, I think. As soon as the time is right, I'm tossing him over the balcony and getting to Diane. But I can't say this, so instead, I say, "What if they never show up? What if we starve? We only have so much vending machine food." "He's right," Abby says. "Can it, whore," Pat says. "Less of the talking, and more moving." Ryan and I pass Abby and Kevin as we head back to the almost barren weight room.

I catch eyes with her, see the fire in them. Kevin just looks defeated, it's a terrible look on such a gladiator, but I guess he has every right to be. The rack where the dumbbells used to be is empty. Large, hunks of metal with three rows for weights from two pounds to a hundred pounds. "Come on," I say. "Let's get this one." Ryan shakes his head. "Watch out, Glass. Let the real men handle this." I cock my head. Real men? I don't remember seeing this asshole bashing in the zombies ten minutes ago. Whatever. I'll let him do his thing. No way will he be able to move it by himself. It's got to be about three hundred pounds of pure steel. "Unlike you, I've lifted heavy shit before," Ryan says. "I don't just sit behind a desk all day and make up stupid stories." He sounds bitter, but it's cool. "Go right ahead," I say with a smile. He struggles at first, his pale face going beet red. To my surprise, he actually lifts one end of the rack up so it's pointing straight up to the ceiling. "Now what?" I ask, trying not to laugh. "You gonna roll it all the way to the steps." Ryan's breathing heavily, half-hunched over, sweat standing out on his forehead. "Yeah," he says. "Maybe I will.

Get out of here and make yourself useful, Glass." He starts to push against the metal again. It easily towers over him by about five feet. I cringe as it topples, expecting the noise to be like a lightning bolt at my feet, but it doesn't topple over the way Ryan intends it to. It topples over on him. I jump toward him as quick as I can. His arms catch the middle rack, but it's too much force. This close, I can hear the bones grinding inside of him to keep him from being smashed.

I have the top rack in hand, the metal edge slicing into my flesh, causing me to bite my tongue. "Fuck fuck fuck fuck," Ryan is saying. This is much worse than my run in with the bench press. So much worse. I don't give up. I give it all I've got. In one strong push, I give Ryan enough room to let go and dive out of the way. This means all the force of the rack he was holding up comes crashing into my palms, and it's too much. I grunt and scream. Somewhere, dumbbells crash to the floor as George, the closest one, runs over to us. "Go, Ryan!" I yell. And he tries.

The weight is just too much. I let go before it takes me down with it. The rack comes crashing down with all the force of an angry god. I think the floor will crack open and we'll wind up falling through. Then I hear Ryan scream out. I've fallen away, landing on my ass, my head spinning from lack of oxygen in my struggle to hold the rack up, vision blurry. But my vision isn't blurry enough to miss what has happened to Ryan's leg. The rack caught him in the middle of the shin. His khakis are torn open. White skin is smeared with red blood. His scream should be louder, but I think he's just in too much shock. George tries to lift the rack up, barely raising it a few inches off of Ryan's leg. I scramble up to help. By this time, Kevin and Abby are helping, too.

Miss Seton and Pat are nowhere to be seen, but I'm not looking for them. With Kevin helping, we easily get the rack off of Ryan. Abby helps pull him out from under it. "Fuck, fuck," Ryan says. His hands are over his face, tears stream down his cheeks. "It's broken, isn't it?" I look to the wound. It's worse than broken. It's almost amputated. I can see the bone in the sea of broken flesh and blood. It's not broken cleanly but rather splintered. We need to get him to the hospital. "Uh," Abby says. She's at a loss for words. We all are.

Ryan looks down at the wound, peeking through his splayed-out fingers on his face. His eyes show white and he falls over, passed out. I hate to admit it, but I feel bad for the kid. I should've helped, shouldn't have let him try to do that on his own. Something bad was going to happen. It always seems to be that way. Over the quiet shaky breathing, I hear footsteps. I turn to see Pat strolling through. No concern written on his face, only curiosity. When he sees the blood dripping onto the rubber floor, Pat raises the gun. "No!" I shout. I grab his forearm, and I think the act alone shocks him.

He pulls free of my grip. "What are you doing? Don't you see?" Pat screams. "He'll just weigh us down." I know I can't reason with him. So I do something I never thought I'd do for an asshole like Ryan. I stand in front of him, put my body between the gun and the end of his life. Kevin follows, then Abby, and then, reluctantly, George. "You'll have to kill us all if you're gonna get to him, Pat," Abby says. I smile. I don't want to jump the gun, but it's safe to call these people my friends, I think. Even, if it's the shortest friendship of all time.

Zombie apocalypses have a way of doing that. Pat lowers the gun, shakes his head. "You're all crazy. You know that?" He sticks it in the back of his waistband. "Fine, do what you have to do, but leave me out of it. When I'm right, when this little bastard is the cause of your demise because you're stuck dragging him around like a two-legged dog, I'll be there to say I told you so. Now get that damn barricade built." He leaves the weight room. As I watch him go, I see Miss Seton looking on with a pained expression. Her whole world is crumbling. "There's a first aid kit in the cardio section," Abby says after a moment of silence. "Nothing much, band aids, gauze, disinfectant. We can wrap up the wound, try to splint it. I don't know." "Let's get it," I say. I look to Kevin and George. "You guys keep an eye on him?" They both nod. "Fuck that man's barricade," George says loud enough for Pat to hear.

Pat watches from near the drinking fountains at the top of the steps. The shadows from the moderately-high pile of gym equipment we've put together shroud his face, but they don't hide the venom in his eyes. "Shit," Abby says. She throws a bunch of balled up papers and other useless junk from an open drawer at a desk near the back of the cardio area. It's so desolate up here. From where I stand, I can barely see the group. Kevin looks huge even from here. He kneels near Ryan. George paces back and forth with his arms crossed. Miss Seton has her head in her hands. I reckon she's crying but I can't hear her sobs over the pounding from the first floor, from the snarls and clawing dead hands against the metal doors. "Where is it? Where is it?" Abby is saying. She looks up at me with wet eyes. "He's a dick, yeah, but we can't just quit. We can't just let him die. Like, not even try." "I know," I say.

She slams the top drawer closed, then rips open the one underneath it. A handful of stopwatches bounce off the rubber floor. A box of blue pens falls next. "He needs medical attention," I say. "Band-Aids and Neosporin aren't going to save him." It's sad, but it's true. Besides, there's a bigger problem here. "How? By killing all those things outside, driving right up to the hospital? Killing all those people I know, the ones who went to my school, the teachers, mailmen...my friends?" "No," I say. "We need to get rid of Pat." She stops, looks up at me with a frown on her face. "Like...kill him?" I don't answer immediately. I let the silence hang there for a moment.

See, I don't know if that's what I mean when I say we need to get rid of Pat. He's unstable, that much is true, not to mention that he's a complete and total asshole. Now that Abby's put words in my mouth, I think to myself that maybe it isn't actually a bad idea. We could make it look like an accident, a suicide or something. Even jump him and throw him to the flesh eaters. You know, just in case the world is righted sooner than we think. I realize I am angry, I am just out for blood so I don't tell her any of this. Instead, I say, "Look what he did to Earl. That wasn't human.

That was something only a monster can do. Now he's holding us hostage." She stands up straighter, still a head shorter than me, but looks me dead in the eyes. "He stepped up, that's all he did. Pat isn't a bad man. I've known him for almost three years. He's here five days a week. It's the predicament we're in. It's changing us. Besides, if we...do that to Pat, it makes us as bad as he is. "Ryan can be saved. He's not dead yet, yes!" She smiles as she pulls out a blood-red first aid kit. It looks like it's older than the both of us combined, but when she opens it up, the contents are new. Probably some yearly mandated law to keep it updated or something.

There's, a handful of bandages in all different sizes, some aspirin, cloth tape, wet wipes, cortisone ointment, peroxide, gauze pads, tweezers, a thermometer, purple latex gloves, and a little booklet straight from the seventies. There's also a flashlight and spare batteries. Where the heck was this thing when Freddy Huber decked me in the face? "Come on," Abby says. A sliver of hope fills my chest. The first aid kit is more stocked than I'd imagined. If we could keep him alive for the night, I'm sure the help will come in the morning. But the problem is, what if someone else gets hurt or sick? It doesn't matter, I guess, because I don't plan on staying the night here.

I plan on sleeping with Diane, like I always do, after I save her. Still, I keep my mouth shut as we approach the group again. Not much has changed except for Ryan is awake now. He looks delirious, near death.

Kevin stares at the floor, sitting cross-legged. "We got the kit," Abby says. "Miss Seton, come over and help us." "That won't be necessary," Pat says, walking over to us from his sentry post near the drinking fountains. Ryan groans. He shakes his head back and forth. Sweat drips from his face. "No, no..." he says. Miss Seton drops down to one knee and starts rummaging through the kit. She pulls the tiny bottle of peroxide out from beneath the bandages. "Stop it," Pat says to her. "We ain't killing him," George says. "It's pointless!" Pat screeches. "Look at that leg." My hands clamp Ryan around the shoulders, pressing him up against the wall. Pat stands over us, gun raised.

Downstairs, the sounds of the dead are amplified. A metal bar falls over, bounces. "They're in!" George says. I get up to see for myself. Through the grates in the guardrail, I see the shadowy figures of people stumbling over the debris barricade. Another of Kevin's makeshift barriers falls over, a group of snarling freaks with it. The weight was too much, and instead of trying to find a way out of here, we are now just sitting ducks. Thanks a lot, Pat. Your good measure has killed us all. A man in a suit or what was once a man leads the way.

One of his eyes is completely gouged out, a river of blood trickles from his ducts. A large chunk of ear is missing on his left side. His necktie is as ruined as his sunken-in face. More follow his lead. They can't use the steps, no way. I think this because they couldn't figure out how to open the front doors. They had just knocked against the glass until they accidentally triggered the handicap automatic door opener. I look over to Ryan. He's started screaming. His mouth is nothing but a black cave with white stalactites for teeth.

Miss Seton pours the peroxide on the wound. Pat has the gun out in front of him. His arm shakes, no, his whole body shakes. I think he might pull the trigger, I really do. But Kevin shoots up from my side. He whizzes past me. Pat catches the big guy lumbering over out of the corner of his eye and lowers the weapon. All he can do is stare with wide eyes. "I need to clean the wound, Ryan, honey," Miss Seton is saying in a soothing voice. "It'll be better once I clean it."

Kevin drops down, puts two big mitts against Ryan to stop his bucking. "Towel," he says to Abby. "Give me a towel." He then leans his forearm across Ryan's chest like a safety bar on some demented rollercoaster. The towel turns into a ball in Kevin's hand, then when Ryan opens his mouth to scream again, he shoves it in. The screams are still loud but muted. I risk another glance over the guardrail. The creeps file in like ants heading to a picnic. "Come on," George says. He has a dumbbell in hand, twenty pounds, and he cocks it back behind his head and throws the thing like it only weighs five pounds.

The guy with the missing ear takes it full in the face. When it hits him, it doesn't explode his skull into a million gushy pieces. It just stuns him, and he stops for a second. He even looks down at the shiny metal of the dumbbell. "Need more weight than that," I say. George rolls his arm in a circle. "You try heaving that shit," he says. "I'd like to keep my rotator cuffs intact." "Well, I'd like to keep my guts," I say. I pick up a five-pound plate, throw it like a Frisbee, aiming at the guy with the bitten ear. I miss terribly, and the plate goes flying into one of the doors that still has most of its glass.

The glass explodes in a burst of glittering shards. Hands and legs and dead faces pop through. "Nice one, Glass," George says. He has another dumb bell, and he waits until the things are almost at the first step where Earl's body lays. "Wait," I say to George. "Don't. You have to look away. Look away." "Huh?" And just like I expected, the things don't keep coming once they stumble upon Earl's body. I think I even see one of them smile, but I know it's just my imagination. "Aw, hell no," George says. He throws the dumbbell anyway.

# Chapter Sixteen

He's bent down picking another one up before the first one hits. "Stay away from him, you assholes," he screams. I grab his arm. "Stop, we might need those if they break through the barricade." "We have a gun!" George says. "Shoot them, Pat. Shoot them!" "Shut the hell up," Pat says. I look at him and he doesn't even notice what's going on. He's too invested in whatever Miss Seton is doing to Ryan's leg wound.

Down at the bottom of the steps, Earl is nothing but a squished head and an open, torn-up body. The zombies are all on their knees, clawing at the flesh, lapping at the sea of blood. Their hands are rakes. They're up to their elbows in organs and guts. A low rattling comes from the back of their throats as they open their mouths to dig in to what was once the old man. George stands there with his mouth hung open, waiting for Pat to do something. When he doesn't, George turns back to the pile of dumbbells and chucks them down the steps. He's like a rapid-fire, machine gun. Blurs of gray. Shiny plates fill and leave his hands. Screw the rotator cuffs. Most of the dead don't notice when the dumbbells hit them, or when the plates bounce off of their skulls. They're too invested in the dinner they're smearing all over the steps.

The last thing George throws is a pink weight that weighs about three pounds. It barely makes it to the horde, bounces off a step then lands in the middle of Earl's open stomach. Three heads pop up to follow the trajectory of the weight. A Woman, snarls at me looking at them over the fence. Her teeth are gone. I can't imagine she'd have much success in the feast going on down there, and maybe she's smart enough to realize that, too. Because she stands up all slow and deliberate, fresh blood running off of her chin, and looks me right in the eyes.

Each step is laborious and pained, but she moves up the stairs without much difficulty. Her snarling grows louder, then she's pushing up against the treadmills and ellipticals, making them creak. I look to

Pat, feeling a mixture of hate and anxiety. It would really be nice to have that gun in my hand right about now, but we're trapped up here and all I have are a couple dumbbells too heavy for me to lift, a dude about to die, and stir-crazy partners.

Ryan's towel falls out of his mouth, and the screams cut through the air. "Shut him up!" Pat says. Kevin tries to hold him as Abby fumbles with the towel. There's a disgusting look on her face as she picks it up. It's covered in blood and spit. Miss Seton wraps the leg tight, red already seeping through the gauze. "Yo, Pat, a little help here," I say. He turns, mouth half-open and ready to make a snarky comment, but looks past me at the shambling woman. When I turn, I see more than the woman. Now a couple more have joined her.

The people snacking on Earl don't even look up. Innards stretch then snap between their teeth. Guts hang from the corner of their mouths. The three coming up the step have found the fresh meat. Hands beat the plastic casing of the treadmill. They're stronger than I originally thought because I'm leaning up against the other side of the treadmill and each time they hit it, I'm pushed a fraction of an inch forward. Ryan's screams are to the point of glass-shattering. Miss Seton fidgets. "Almost done," she says. "Hold on, honey." "Kevin, help me!" I yell. "I can't hold it by myself." George helps, too, but only by throwing things at the shambling corpses. The short distance must be easier on his arms because I hear bones shatter, then a body roll down the steps.

Kevin comes over, presses his big shoulder into the treadmills. "We could really use that gun," I say to Pat. But he doesn't answer. He just stares wide-eyed at the kid on the ground. The one who doesn't look like much of a kid or a human for that matter. He looks like he is dying, and so will we if we don't do anything. Screw this, I think. I don't owe these people anything. I will not be killed by their stupidity. I will not go down with this sinking ship. If help was going to come, it would've already come by now.

I have Diane to worry about, not Pat Huber and Ryan the douche bag janitor. "Abby! Take me to the roof," I yell. She arches an eyebrow, but otherwise ignores me. Her hands are on Ryan's arm. "Abby, come on! We aren't going to defend this place, we have to go." "I'm with Glass," George hollers. He grunts as he throws a twenty-five pound plate like a frisbee. I don't see where it lands, but I hear the snarls rip through the air at the bottom of the stairs as if he disturbed their dining experience.

He turns to Kevin: "Let's go, big guy. We need to get out of here. Can't hold that all night," he says. Veins bulge from Kevin's biceps. I rush over to help while the rest of them get ready to go. From around the corner, a man with a dislocated jaw, shambles up the railing. He reaches a hand out toward me. His jaw opens to expose bloody teeth. Then he falls. Right over the railing, about thirty feet and lands on his stomach with a splat near the running track. Something shoots off his face, dancing across the rubber floor. I watch this all with laser focus. I don't know why, but it entrances me.

When whatever it is stops spinning, I see it. It's his jaw, completely unhinged, disconnected from his face. He turns over to look up at me hanging over the railing. Bloody hands reach toward the ceiling. A sound like a broken sprinkler escapes the gaping, black hole. I thought I was a horror writer, I thought I was an architect of nightmares. I was wrong. This is truly a nightmare, one I had no hand in creating or controlling.

"What about Ryan?" Abby asks. They're all standing now. Kevin still has his back pressed up against the stairway barricade. Every five seconds or so, his soles squeak from the dead pushing, trying to get in. "Leave him," Pat says. The way he speaks chills me. "No, don't leave him," I say. "Kevin, can you carry him?" Kevin nods. I may have told Abby that whatever happens to Ryan is out of our hands now, that the real problem was Pat, but I've never been so wrong. After seeing the zombie without the jaw, seeing the things eating Tony's corpse, eating Earl's, I know I've never been more wrong.

We can't let that happen to Ryan. He's a dick, but not even someone like him deserves a fate as terrible as that. "T-Tell my mom I'm gonna stay the night at Robbie's. Tell her I'm gonna miss dinner," Ryan murmurs. His head rolls from shoulder to shoulder. He's sweating more now. Delirium is settling in. "We will, Ry, we will," Abby says, trying to comfort him. "I'll try to run. I won't hold you guys back. Please, just help me. I don't want to die like Earl. Please," Ryan says. "I got you, kid," Kevin says. "Come on, let's go." "Wait, everyone grab a weapon," I say.

I walk over to the small cache of dumbbells and barbells. I grab a ten pounder that has a hexagonal shape on each end. Sharp and, hard. The others follow my lead. Every-one except Kevin and Pat. Miss Seton holds a dainty, pink two pounder. George has a twenty. Abby picks up a weighted bar, you know, one of the shorter ones with the rubber padding and colors on each end. It can't be more than eight pounds. "Lead the way," I say to her.

Abby takes a deep, shaky breath. Blinks fast. "On the count of three," I say to Kevin because as soon as he moves, that barricade is going to topple over and the dead are going to spill over it all, hell-bent on feasting on us. He flexes his whole body as he gives one last shove backward. "How 'bout on the count of two! Can't hold it much longer." "One...two...three...now!" He dives out of the way of the falling exercise equipment. Then he scoops Ryan up like a baby.

Abby points us toward the aerobic area. She runs faster than I'd expect her to run. I don't see the dead, but I hear them. Their hands scratching at the plastic, knocking the weight plates together. I risk a glance. There's about five of them who made it over the barrier. The noise is drawing more, and they lumber up the stairs, still hungry. The zombies coming up the steps wear masks of blood over their mouths. It's almost sickening, almost enough to make me keel over and vomit. If this is how the world is now, will I ever get used to it? I don't think so, but I think about Diane and how the only way I'll be able to survive is with her by my side.

I couldn't go on without her. She's the reason I haven't given up yet. She's what gives me hope. "Carly! Come on," George says. One of his hands grips my arm. I didn't even realize it. I was transfixed, just standing there, staring at the carnage, at the freaks. Fingernails dig into my skin, and he pulls me. I almost drop the ten-pound weight I hold in my hand like a hammer. The dead lumber toward us. They're only about five feet away when George nearly yanks me off my feet. Abby is in the lead. She's almost to the fence that separates the aerobic area from the basketball spectator stands.

Pat is behind her, Miss Seton behind Pat, and last is Kevin with Ryan in his arms. Abby weaves through treadmills. "Around the corner," she says. "It's a service stairway." Snarls crawl up my back, almost drowning out Abby's voice. "Carly, watch out!" Abby says. I turn around to see a zombie with his nose half-ripped off, lunging at me. I don't even think. I just act, let the dumbbell come down on its face. There's a sickening crunch of bones shattering. My shoulder is nearly ripped out. A pinch in my back travels from my ass to my neck. But No-Nose drops like a sack of bricks. Bash one head in, two more take their place, I guess, because an old woman and an old man, both more like skeletons than recently dead people don't even take notice to their fallen comrade.

A hand goes for my throat. I fall over, losing my weapon. Rotten skin and dusty bones fills my nostrils, then the damn thing opens its mouth. My forearm goes up to block the thing's bite. Problem is my forearm is bare. One bite and I'm the next nameless corpse. What a bittersweet irony that would be. The writer becoming the monster he writes about. I drive my elbow into its neck. The one on top of me is the man. His wife joins in on the fun. This is not how I picture my first threesome.

I use my other arm to try to fend her off, but somehow she's stronger than he is. Fresher maybe, too. George screams. There's a crack that follows that scream. I'm showered in a cloud of dust and brains. Some wet stuff, too, like blood or God knows what else. Another crack. The old guy drops on me, unmoving. "Come on," George says. He pulls me out from beneath the lifeless corpses, but more are on the way. I can't sit around stunned. I have to move. Their eyes are yellow, some are red. All are dead. "Come on, you assholes, we can't wait around all night," Pat says.

He has his gun raised, but he won't fire. There are too many, not enough bullets. He might be a good shot, who knows? He knows he can't drop all twenty or so that come up the steps. I cross the gate and slam it shut. It's only about waist high, but it might slow the bastards down. We weave through a maze of stationary bikes and treadmills. Dead TVs hang above us, watching this carnage unfold with black-screened eyes. The gate bangs open not long after I'm through. Abby and Pat turn the corner, knifing through the top part of the basketball stands. I'm sweating, I can feel it, but something else leaves my skin, too. It's dread. I really hate heights.

This recreation center is full of heights. Who knows how high up we'll be, and if we'll ever really be high enough to get away from these things? George throws his dumbbell in one last-ditch effort to slow them down. It whistles by my head, nails a woman in her stomach. She doubles over and falls. The others take no notice of the momentary roadblock. They aren't stopping. All I can do is turn back around, and run. Kevin and Ryan turn the corner that Abby and Pat have just turned. George and I are right there. I go first. There's a clatter. Kevin's deep voice rings out. "Fuck," he says. I trip over the big guy like he's a fallen boulder. Ryan sprawls out in front of him curled up in a ball, moaning, grabbing at his leg which just kind of hangs there like rubber. George slows up before he's the next victim in this dumbass pileup. He hops over Kevin, clamps a hand around the big guy's forearm and tries to pull. With me he had no problem, but Kevin probably weighs twice what I weigh.

I scramble up and try to help. My eyes bulge out of my face as I pull with all of my might. Kevin shakes his head, lifts his face up. He wears a mask of red over his left eyebrow, even more blood on the floor where he hit. He pushes himself up, dazed. The snarls grow louder, that dry clicking noise in the back of the zombies' throats. A gray-skinned girl is the first around the corner. I swear her eyes light up when she sees the meal at her feet. She wastes no time in dropping down on Kevin's bare legs. Her mouth clicks open. Black spit rolls from the corners of her lips in thick, ropy goops. I kick out and hit her square in the face.

Her hair flies back as if she's being electrocuted. The spit sprays, dotting the white walls to my right. "Go! Go!" I say to Kevin. But he moves like a drunk. George kicks another one in the chest. Sends the bastard over the railing to our left and into the bleachers where it gets tangled. "Too many!" George shouts. "Go, we have to go!" I try to block it out, try to deafen myself to the guy's logic, but sometimes I'm too stupid for my own good.

I kick at another's head. It falls in a spray of blood and brains, the soft, mushy skin not standing a chance. One grapples at me, but I see it from the corner of my eyes and dip, throwing an elbow into its back, sending it to the bleachers with its friend. "Carly! Come on!" Teeth are inches from my face. My fist goes up, hits the man under his jaw. His runny, black eyes close with the force of it. "Kevin!" I yell. But it's too late. He screams out as one of the things dig into his calf. Tendons and skin pop and snap. A ringing fills my head. It's not real. None of this can be real. In one last kick, I free up enough space for me to back out, to hop over Kevin's body. The rest of them fall down on him. They cover him like ants on a dropped piece of food.

I get about ten feet away from the carnage, from the spraying blood and the crunching sounds of jaws working at his flesh, when he lifts up. This muscular man I once called a friend in high school actually does a half-pushup with about ten dead bodies crawling over him. It doesn't last long. He falls back to the floor with a crash. The look he gives me will probably give me nightmares for the rest of my life assuming the rest of my life lasts as long as I want it to. It's a look of pain, of defeat. Kevin reaches an arm out toward us as he lifts his head, then drops, his bloody face bouncing off the linoleum.

George has Ryan in his arms. "Come on, man!" he shouts. The last thing I hear as I crawl up the steps are Kevin's dying screams. He dies a hero.

# Chapter Seventeen

Pat's face almost fills the opening at the top of the metal ladder. Behind him is an expanse of black sky dotted with white pinpricks of light. I love the stars. They remind me of Diane. The late nights in England, where we get drunk off cheap wine and sit on the balcony, looking at these very stars. Even in the winter when her body keeps me warmer than any fire. I'm smiling as I think this, as my heart aches for her. I'm trying not to think of her in some back alley covered in trash and blood with inhuman hands digging into her insides. It's a hard job.

They say your life flashes before your eyes when you're about to die. There have been a few occasions tonight where I've had that feeling, except it's not my childhood or my memories. All I see is Diane's smiling face. So beautiful. So perfect. "Nuh-uh, drop the kid," Pat says, bringing me back down to earth. He's not talking to me, he's talking to George. "What the fuck do you mean drop him?" "You know exactly what I mean." "This is a human life we're talking about," I say. "He might be one of the last ones for all we know.

We have to keep him alive." "What did I say about talking back to the man with the gun?" Pat says. He flashes the pistol which gleams in the starlight. "And there is seven billion people on this planet. You think Ryan the janitor is going to be one of the last ones? You think the fate of the human race is going to have to rely on this shit-stain?" "Man, fuck your gun. I'll come up there and beat your ass right now," George says. "Patrick," Miss Seton says in her most motherly voice. "Let them up!" Pat's face drains of all color. "Yeah, shit-stain," Abby says from the roof.

She's not visible. He exhales a deep breath, then rolls his eyes. "Fine," he says as he moves out of the hatch. Thank God, because those snarls and choking, gurgling sounds drift up the hall. It's haunting. George goes first. He hangs Ryan over his shoulder like a backpack. "You gotta hold on, kid," George says to him. Ryan moans something that isn't decipherable, but his hands clasp together around George's neck. "I'm right behind you," I say, then turn my head away from the two, watching the corner, waiting for one of the dead to lunge at me. I won't hesitate anymore. I am changed. I am Carly Zombie Slayer.

I am a twisted creation from the depths of my own imagination. Nothing comes. The coast is clear. I shamble up the ladder, careful not to let Ryan fall off of George's back. There are only about ten steps. It doesn't take us too long to reach the cool, night air. Abby closes the hatch, stands over it like it's an animal she just accidentally hit with her car. "You don't think they can climb up the ladder, do you?" I shake my head. "If they can't figure out how to pull the lobby doors open, I think we'll be okay."

I almost tell her that according to my rules, there's not a chance in hell they can, but this isn't my fictional world. Her mouth forms a thin line. "I hope so, I really hope so." Something about her face tells me she doesn't believe a word I say. With the sounds of the horde secure behind the hatch, it hits me how quiet it is outside, how still and...empty. The darkness is a complete black for as far as the eye can see in front of me. No streetlights are on. No headlights driving down the road. All we have is God's natural light above us, and it's not much. There's a smell in the air. A, rotten smell. "Now what?" George says. He's lying on his back. Ryan is next to him, unmoving, but making soft whimpering sounds through his nose. The leg wound spills blood at a steady rate.

The gauze is almost soaked through. Miss Seton rummages through the first aid kit a few feet away from the both of them. I'm standing, breathing calmer than earlier. Abby is next to me, pacing a few feet back and forth. Pat's back is to us all. He looks out toward the darkness, where, far up the road, is the Leering Research Facility, Pat Huber's former place of employment, first, thanks to a fire and now, thanks to the dead rising. "We wait up here," Abby says, answering George. "What else can we do?" I nod. "Shit," George says, then he does a sit-up, straining. "None of y'all was bit, were you?" I pat myself down, then shake my head.

If I was bit, I think I'd know. "Nope," Abby says. "Never got close to them...wait a minute, where's Kevin?" I shake my head. I hoped this wouldn't come up, that everyone would've forgotten about him because it hurts to say this out loud. "H-He didn't make it, Abby." "What? You're joking, right?" "I wish I was," I say. "The damn things fell on him. He tripped carrying Ryan, and they were on him faster than I could believe," George says. I bow my head, pinch my nose. "We tried, Abby. We really tried, there were just way too many of them." "A couple seconds longer and we wouldn't have made it, either," George says.

She sniffles, then explodes into a sob. "God, why? What the hell is going on? Why is this happening to us? I'm not a bad person. We aren't bad people, are we?" "Don't question God," Miss Seton snaps. "We are beneath him. We have no right in questioning his motives." I think she's right, but I keep my mouth shut. Doesn't matter why this is happening or who had a hand in it. It's happening, and all we can do is survive. I have to, God or not, for Diane. "It wasn't God or the Devil," Pat says. His back is still facing us and he talks in a quiet voice. "This is man-made. We did this." "What? How you know?" George asks.

Pat turns around. His face is still white, gun still in his hand. "It was an accident," he says. "You think it was an accident?" I ask. Pat shrugs. "They were studying a virus...at Leering. I worked on the third floor, dealing with animal testing mostly, but I heard the rumors. Test Subject 101. They said she came back to life except she was supposed to be a he and the project head was bat-shit crazy. When things went south, one of the researchers made it out of the decontamination chamber with a bite wound. He went a few places, spreading the virus before he could be quarantined, not thinking in his right mind." He sighs. "Yeah, I heard the rumors, but I didn't believe them. Then there was the fire. Fires happen from time to time. There was talk of rebuilding, of renovation. That fire was an accident, I was sure, especially when they shut us down. You know, all kinds of bat-shit things make the rounds at Leering, and so far none proved to be true...until now. "When they shut us down, I was relieved.

Six months away from early retirement and a nice, fat pension. Relieved. But I wasn't thinking it was because we were all royally fucked. I wasn't thinking the Leering big-wigs saw their fuck-up and decided to jump ship, leaving us all to crash and burn. No, I wasn't thinking any of that. Besides, I heard all of this almost six months ago. A lot can go through a man's mind in six months." A heavy silence hangs in the air. This is bullshit. I don't believe Pat. He knew this whole time. He was never in denial. He was probably the cause of this whole thing.

That wouldn't surprise me. Leave it up to a Huber to end the world. "If the government broke it, they will most surely fix it, won't they?" Miss Seton asks. "Honey, I don't know," Pat says. "A virus like this is like wildfire. It'll burn and burn until it eventually extinguishes itself or...until it consumes everything in its path." "Will we catch it?" Miss Seton asks, somehow her face going paler. "If we haven't caught it yet, I'd say we're immune. Since the rumors are turning out to be true, what we're seeing here is an exploding time bomb.

Everyone exposed was exposed at roughly the same time, and now the virus is changing them all at roughly the same time," Pat answers. I see the seriousness in his face and think back to my own zombie novel. The cause of the dead rising was from some crazy spaceship that crash landed in an abandoned Scottish cornfield, chock full of little green men infected with radioactive alien parasites. Outlandish, yes. Pat's so-called rumors are not as outlandish. Miss Seton relaxes a bit, but I don't. "Roughly," Pat repeats. "Which could mean we're not out of the clear yet.

We could turn now, we could turn later. Give it another month for us. Maybe longer for Glass, being an out-of-towner and all. Even longer for the rest of the world." He smiles at me like he's enjoying all of this. "So you're telling us you knew about all of this and you didn't do anything?" I ask. Another typical Huber trait. "This whole time, you knew a bite could be fatal? You knew Burnett was going to turn into one of those things? In the back of your mind, you knew." "They were rumors, kid! I really didn't want to believe them. Would you believe horse-shit like that? No! That's the type of stuff you block out. Trust me, what I saw today is going to haunt me forever," he says. "But it's not my fault.

Sometimes you play with fire and sometimes you melt your face off." "Sure," I say. "Man, don't listen to this fool. He's just blowing smoke out his ass," George says to me. Abby is sitting now, her face in her hands. Pat just shrugs, walks over to her, and puts his hand on her shoulder. "Hey, don't get hung up on the big guy. One less person to worry about, right? Those things will be so full when they're done with him, a big guy like Kevin...it'll be a buffet. They won't even want us after him." "Stop," I say. My knuckles crack as I ball up my hands. I've had enough of this prick. Gun or not, I'm going to shut him up if he doesn't shut himself up.

Abby doesn't answer with anything besides her sobs. "I think its Judgment Day," Miss Seton says in the tone of someone revealing a dark secret. "Oh, please," Pat says. "No, no, this is God's wrath. The meek shall inherit the Earth. Those things are the meek" "Then what are we?" Abby snaps, causing me to jump. "We are still here. There's got to be tons of people still here. This is new. It would take forever for the population to be wiped out." "Cry baby has a point," Pat says. "Enough! Stop it, Pat," Abby says.

Black streaks run from her eyes, then they smear as she wipes them away with the back of her hand. "He wants to make us suffer. We have wronged Him," Miss Seton says. She tilts her head up to the sky, outstretches her arms. "But I have not. I am your humble and honest servant. I've done nothing but spread your love for all of my years. I am forever grateful for the life you have blessed me with. Please, do not take it now." When she opens her eyes, there's a sparkle of tears. Pat laughs. "Yeah, make good with him as soon as the shit hits the fan.

Don't forget to ask for forgiveness for all that money you stole a few months back." Miss Seton's face freezes. Her eyes slowly grow wider. "Yeah, I heard about that. It's not like it was a secret. Everyone knew, even Tony. He just felt bad for you. After your husband died, he said you got a couple screws knocked loose." "I-I" she stammers. "Am a thief," Pat says. "Feels good to come clean, huh? Why don't we all come clean? Here, I'll go first. Let's see, well, I've been married for twenty-five years. Not one of those years has been a faithful year. Hookers, Interns, Lab assistants, Wild weekends in Vegas with a couple buddies. She knows, too, but she's too afraid to leave me. Thinks she'll be stuck on her own with our dumbass kid.

I mean he's almost thirty and still lives at home. What a fucking disappointment." He laughs like a maniac. "You know what? Since we're coming clean, I don't love that bastard. It's my own damn fault. I stayed away from him like he was the plague. Now guess what? There's an actual plague! Life's funny like that." I've never seen someone break down before, not in real life. It's hard to watch, but at the same time, it's entertaining. Knowing Freddy Huber is a momma's boy comforts me. At least I got my own place.

The bastard might have a mean right hook, but I got a two-bedroom apartment. "I love her, you know. I love my wife. She's my best friend. I just...I just get bored. Her tits are saggy. She's wrinkling. I can't remember the last time she shaved her legs," Pat continues. "If I can pop one without a Viagra around her, it's a damned miracle." "Okay, too much information, man," George says. "You don't like it? Then confess, George!" Pat says. "Tell us about your stint in prison or the drug dealers you've popped." "You better cut that shit out," George snaps. "I ain't never been to prison.

I was in the Army. Five years. Saw some action in Iraq..." his voice trails off. He blinks slowly, then brings his hand up to swipe his bald scalp. "Maybe I should be in prison, man. I saw some fucked up things. I did fucked up things. All for what? For some oil? To stop some terrorists? That's five years of my life I ain't never gonna get back. I missed the birth of my kid. I lost the love of my life. Now she won't even let me see the kid. They live in California, all the way across the country." "Good, good," Pat says. "Let it out. Might as well if Miss Seton is right and God is listening. Come clean and we'll be saved, right?" She ignores him, just stares straight ahead of her, past me and Abby. "How about you, Glass? What do you got to come clean about?" Pat asks me. He's smiling, and the gun is still in his hand. My eyes scan over it. He sees me do it, then flashes it to me. Everyone looks either stunned or deep in thought with the exception of Ryan who's taken to a slight variation of the death rattle.

His eyes are open, but I don't think he sees much. "I don't have anything to get off of my chest," I say. "Bullshit. Anything, Glass. A toy you stole in kindergarten. The fat kid you used to pick on in high school." He's trying to get a rise out of me, but I won't let him. "I killed my cat when I was younger," Abby says. Her words are like a slap in the face to us all. Even Miss Seton is shaken out of her pouty trance. Ryan stirs, too, but I don't think it was because of what Abby said. I think he's just in so much pain. "He liked to climb the tree behind the shed in my backyard.

I liked to climb it, too. I was always scared to go past a certain point. It was really high, like maybe fifty feet, I don't know, but as a nine-year-old, that's like a million stories. My friend said cats always land on their feet. One day, that dumb cat was up there so high, I wanted to save him. I wanted to be like the firefighters in the movies and stuff. So I did it. I got all the way up there, but he wouldn't let go of the bark.

He was glued to it with his nails, I tried and tried to pry him free. Finally, he gave in. But there was no way I was climbing back down with him in my hand, and Shelly said cats always landed on their feet." She cringes. Fidgets a bit with the memory fresh inside of her head. "I tossed him off. He didn't...he didn't die instantly. But he broke all of his legs when he hit the concrete, and he was bleeding internally. My mom had to take him to one of those emergency vets. They said he was suffering. I named him Simba even though he was black, you know, like from The Lion King. Simba had to be put down.

I never said I threw him. I said he jumped or fell, I don't know. No one knows about this but me, and now you guys. God, I'm a piece of shit," she says and breaks into another burst of tears. Pat stands there with his mouth hanging wide open. "Wow. Now I'm stuck on a roof with not only a war criminal, a thief, and an adulterer, but also a cat killer. Jesus Christ, today is my lucky day." "It was an accident!" Abby cries. "I was only nine." "Bullshit. Nine-year-olds aren't that stupid." She nods as if Pat is right. Seeing that leaves a bad taste in my mouth. "All right, Glass, try to top that one," Pat says. He crosses his arms and stares at me.

The rest of them stare, too, as if it's expected of me to confess my sins. All their eyes just show the whites. The peer pressure is real, but I'm not a bad person. Am I? I have nothing to contribute. Of course, that's what all the bad people tell themselves: I'm not a bad person. I never fantasized about killing all the assholes who picked on me as a kid, never thought about raiding my grandpa's basement gun rack for something small enough for me to hide in my backpack, never thought about storming Mrs. Grant's sophomore homeroom and making Freddy Huber eat lead. Yeah, that's right, Pat, your own damn son and his stupid friends, too. No, I'm a good person.

"Come clean, Glass, and be saved. Right, Fiona?" Pat says. I don't have to look at him to know that his shit-eating grin is painted on his face like clown's makeup. "It's okay, Carly," Abby says. "We won't judge you." "Speak for yourself, sister," Pat says. "It's nothing..." I say. "Can't be worse than killing people, man," George says. He shakes his head. "That shit will be with me for the rest of my life." I think of Earl. That old man I barely knew. I think of him clawing into the tile floor, shouting for us to help him, for the pain to go away, of his wife winning the Bake-Off. I think of Kevin, of the dead covering him and tearing away at his flesh so I could go on. I think of these things because deep down I blame myself. I could've done something. I could've been better.

We can always be better, even when we say we can't. We can dedicate our lives to improving, but we're too busy thinking of ourselves to do that. Ironic, right? Maybe if I got out and talked to people I'd have friends, but I hate people. I'm too shy. Maybe if I had swung the barbell harder and killed that cowboy hat wearing zombie before he got Earl's leg then he'd still be alive. I could've double-checked. Could've made sure there were no longer any threats. Isn't that what Donnny death slayer would've done? Maybe if I would've never called Kevin, he wouldn't have been here today.

Maybe he'd be at home watching his favorite movie, eating healthy snacks. Maybe if I stayed closer to home, never left my mom, she would still be alive. Maybe she would've quit smoking. Maybe she wouldn't have gone out to Everson's to get that pack of Cigarrettes that ultimately killed her. I say none of this and shrug instead. Because they wouldn't understand. They'd say they do, but they'd never truly understand. That's what makes us different from each other, and I don't mind that one bit. "I guess you'll never be saved then," Pat says.

He turns to Ryan. "What about you, kid?" And Ryan says nothing in return besides letting out a small grunt from between his pursed lips. "Yeah, that's what I thought." There's a silence, an eerie silence that hangs over our heads. Pat tilts his head up to the sky, mocking Miss Seton from earlier. "Well, God...now's the time to save us." Nothing happens. "Thought not. Well, I'm getting the hell off of this roof," Pat says. "I suggest you follow me because I'm the one with the" A thud like a sledgehammer pounding against the hatch cuts him off. Another thud. This one creaks the hinges, lifts the hatch an inch into the air. I see the lines of emergency lights leaking out from the inside. A finger snakes through the crack. It's a bloody finger. The nail hangs off like a tilted crescent moon. Dirty skin. This is the end. There's nowhere to go but off the roof. I see that flash of Diane in my mind's eye again. So vivid. I'm sorry, honey. I'm so sorry.

# Chapter Eighteen

"I thought you said they couldn't climb the ladder!" Abby shouts at me. I was thinking of the zombies from my book, but what the hell did I know? They roll out of the hatch. Bodies and limbs, greasy with Kevin's blood. Their eyes burn yellow and they still look so hungry. Pat aims at the first one to come out and pulls the trigger. It's a woman with hair that may have once been blonde, but the bullet takes off the top half of her head. Brains leak down her sallow skin, staining her face. She slumps forward, dead...again. There's more. They didn't climb the ladder, I'm realizing. There's just so many of them and they're so hungry that they piled up beneath the hatch until they created a mound of zombies which had no choice but to overflow and spill onto the roof. Pat fires again. I don't move as the gun cracks. I swear I can feel the bullet whiz right by my face. This shot is wide and hits the roof with a high-pitched whine. A brief spark lights up the snarling faces. "What do we do? What do we do?" Abby screams.

She cowers behind Pat, who is standing with the gun pointed at the hatch, both hands on the weapon. Another shot goes off. Another spray of blood. The body an older man wearing his navy-blue service outfit falls in just the right place for the others to use him as a stepladder. Three of them spill onto the roof, they get up. Pat pulls off two more shots in quick succession. Both miss their heads. One is struck in the stomach, but that doesn't slow him down.

He lumbers over to me. I've frozen again, a million thoughts racing through my mind. Diane, my mom, my books, my brother, Freddy Huber. I feel like I'm going to explode. "Carly! C'mon," George says. I hear him faintly as if he's yelling at the far end of a long corridor. My ears ring from the gunshots. There's growling and snarling. Wet mouths smacking their lips at me, teeth gnashing. Blood. Darkness. Someone grips me hard. I wince and look up to see George with a twisted look on his face.

He pulls me away, and about a second later, one of the zombies lunge at the spot where I was standing. I shake my head, slowly coming back into the moment. More have broken through the hatch. I count ten on the roof, lumbering to us. Each step they take backs our group up to the edge. We are surrounded by 360 degrees of blacktop with only a faint strip of bushes and shrubs near the front doors. Oh, and we're two stories up. "Fire escape?" I yell at Abby.

She shakes her head. "Anything? Parachute? Trampol " Pat squeezes the trigger, and in the faint ringing and silence between shots, I hear a soft moan. It's not inhuman like these monsters who are coming for our flesh. It's Ryan. He's trying to pull himself up, but he looks so sick, so pained. There's no way that leg will be able to hold him and get him to safety. The monsters are about five feet from him as I make up my mind.

I won't lose him like I lost Kevin. I just won't. I grab him, scooping him up in my arms as best I can. It's not pretty, but it's effective. He shrieks with pain as I do it. Miss Seton and Abby watch me with wide eyes. Pat has a perpetual frown on his face, the gun still up and aiming at the legion of dead behind me. I'm a few steps away from being behind him when he looks at me as if I'm the only one on the roof. The gun follows his gaze. "Drop him," he says. "What?" "Drop the kid, Glass." George keeps looking behind him, seeing how close to the edge they all are. "If you want to live, you will drop the fucking kid." His voice is eerily calm and his eyes mean business.

A couple shades darker and I might confuse him with one of the dead. "Or what?" I say. Pat Huber, just another bully. "Or I shoot you both. I got enough ammunition to do it, son. Don't make me." I don't believe him, and the zombies are too close for me to go anywhere else but forward. Pat doesn't lie. The gun goes off, and my whole body shudders. My eyes jam shut. I think I'm dead, I think a hole in my stomach will start spewing hot blood. It doesn't. Instead, I hear the high thump of skin and bones smacking the roof.

Pat shot one of the things that had gotten too close to me. "Drop him!" he screams. "I don't want to kill you both." I shake my head, and with Ryan in my arms, I walk forward. He'll have to shoot me. Somewhere above us, a cloud moves, revealing white moonlight glinting off the gun's metal. I can see him shaking. Then I see a flash from the muzzle. A bullet whines off of the roof about a foot in front of me. "I mean it, Glass! I'll shoot you both!" He shoots again.

This shot is close enough for me to feel the heat from the slug. But still, I don't slow down. His aim flicks to my right. I turn to look, see a fat woman in a straw hat drop, then the aim is back at me. "Stop!" Abby shouts. My arms shake with the strain of Ryan's weight. I want nothing but to put him down, but I can't. If I do that, they'll be on him like they were on Kevin and Earl. I don't care if that would buy us some time. "Pat, cut the shit," George says. "I'm just trying to save us.

We can't carry around some cripple." "I'm not leaving him behind!" I shout. Ryan moans with pain. His eyes flicker. Chapped lips start to move as if to speak. A weak string of words escape his lips, "T-Thank you," he wheezes. "Carly, look out!" Abby yells. A gnarled hand swipes right by my face. Pat shoots again, and the hand dissolves into a mess of blood and shattered bones. I keep moving, each step a pain. Pat shoots for the last time, and by the pain in my chest, the wrenching fear caused by this close call, I think I've been shot, when really the bullet dings off the roof inches away from my feet. In all the fear, I drop Ryan.

Before I can bend down to pick him up, an older zombie's wispy, white beard turns red with fresh blood and guts. Ryan screams. It's easily the most horrifying sound I've ever heard, worse than Kevin, worse than Tony and Earl. Worse than whatever played in my head when I wrote The Zombie Slayer. I stare in awe pure, utter shock as the others who've made their way onto the roof by way of the dead limb ladder pounce on the poor kid. Intestines stretch like putty from his open stomach before they snap and wind up in between their gnashing teeth. Ryan screams and cries.

The gun goes off, putting an end to his whimpers. His face is not a face anymore. What was once a young man, peach fuzz on his upper lip, acne scars on his cheeks, is now something resembling a stepped-in cherry pie. I failed again. Damn it, I failed again. Someone is behind me. Someone grabs me and yanks me up. "C'mon, kid," George says. "Gotta find a way off of the roof. Gotta go." The dead swarm Ryan's body and they will munch and claw at him until he is nothing...until he is no more. Pat still holds up the gun. He aims at the pile of corpse's wearing tattered clothes, blood and flesh hanging from their chins in goopy strings.

How much time do we have? I wonder. How long before they pick the kid clean? How long until he is nothing but bones? The rage takes me as easily as the fear does, but the rage is louder. Pat sees me coming, so he turns his aim back at my head. He might shoot me. He might end my quest for Diane, but I'm not thinking straight. I cock my fist back, and as it whistles through the air, Pat drops the weapon down to his side. I slug him the same way his son slugged me.

My knuckles crack the loose skin around his jaw, and it feels better than I could ever imagine. He doubles over but doesn't fall. "This is your fault!" I shout. "We could've saved him." "I did the poor bastard a favor." His hand finds the spot where I hit him, fingers swipe away a fresh trickle of blood from the corner of his mouth. "You could learn a thing or two from me, Glass! In this world, the way it is now, you don't have time to think and worry about everyone else. You gotta act, or you gotta die." "Bullshit," I say. "That's just an excuse. No matter what's happened out there, we have to be civilized. We have to protect each other." Pat slowly straightens himself, one hand still clutching the gun, the other holding the spot where I punched him. "And that, my friend, is why you're gonna die," he says, then the gun comes up as he points it straight at my face, and this time, I see the murder in his eyes, I see the underlying cowardice vanish. I see death. Diane, I think as the gun goes off.

The gun doesn't shoot at me, at least I don't think it does because George tackles Pat around the waist as it goes off. I don't see the flash from the muzzle. The bodies are too entwined for that. Miss Seton lets out a scream. George cries out in pain. I rush over to the two men. There's a steady stream of blood pouring out of one of them. I follow the trail, hoping it isn't George. I grab him by the shoulders and roll him off of Pat, and sure enough, George's shirt is slowly soaking through with blood. He clutches at a sizzling hole in his stomach.

Tears and sweat roll down his face. "You shot him!" Abby screams. "You monster, you shot him!" Pat scrambles away from George. I hold the dying man's head in my arms. I've just met the guy, but this hurts. I think of his kid in California, of all things he's going to miss. Again, this should be me, and that thought wrenches my heart. George smiles, blood lining the teeth. "I deserve this, I guess," he says. "All them people I shot and killed overseas.

I deserve this." He looks over to Pat who is now inches from toppling off the roof. "No," I say to George, "you don't. You aren't going to die." He looks at me with a cold calmness in his eyes, then he nods. "Yeah, I am." "I didn't mean to," Pat says. "I was aiming, "For me, yeah, I know," I say. The bastard. Of course I know this. Save your breath. My hands find the bullet wound. I press down on it, trying to stop the blood, but there's so much. It's seeping between my fingers, warm and sticky. George is right, he's going to die. "Look!" Miss Seton says. "Look, they're coming for us!" She shrieks as she points behind me and George.

I risk a glance, and a few of the feasting beasts have turned their dead heads toward the sound of the gunshot. Suddenly, George starts to move in my arms. He grunts as he pulls himself up. I want to hold him down, not let him do what I think he's about to do, but he slips from my grip as if he were made of sand, and I am too stunned. He stands like one of them, hunched over and bloody, his teeth bared. "No," I say. "George, don't!" He takes one look over his shoulders and says, "Get off the roof. Go back home, stay safe, and live, Live!" He plunges into the mob of monsters. A sea of arms takes him. The last part I see before he's gone are the whites of his eyes.

We all stand with our mouths open, hearing the squelching of limbs ripping, of soft screams, of stirring guts. Abby is the first to make a noise, and it's the sound of her quiet sobs. "Well, let's get the fuck off this roof," Pat says. "George sacrificed himself for us. Let's go!" "How?" Miss Seton asks. "How are we going to get off? Sprout wings and fly away?" Abby breaks into the conversation. "We can go back through the hatch," she says, and when she raises her head, I see the gleam of tears in her eyes. At least she's trying to be strong, I think to myself. "Won't work. The whole place is overrun," Pat says. "I don't know how many bullets are left, either. I'm a scientist, not a soldier!" "You shot the soldier!" Abby says.

I hardly hear any of this. There's a rage pumping through my body, causing my ears to ring. I see a flurry of red at the edges of my vision. I'll show you how you can get off the roof. I'll show you, Pat. We're all dead anyway, right? The whole fucking world has gone to hell. Right right right? These thoughts race through my head as my feet pound the rooftop. I'm sprinting in about three steps, coming at Pat like a middle linebacker. I don't even care if he shoots me.

All I want is revenge. At the last second, he realizes what I'm doing. His eyes explode open, his mouth turns into something resembling an O. My hands are out in front of me, hands that have done no wrong, hands that have only killed people in stories, in video games, but now they're ready, eager even, to take a real life. It all happens so fast. My hands crash into his chest. The gun spins out of his grip, whirling and flipping in the air. Faintly, I hear it clatter to the roof, but why is it so faint? Where is the surface I stand on? Suddenly, it's taken out from beneath my feet, and I'm falling. We're both falling. Abby screams, and like the sound of the clattering gun, her screams get more distant the farther we fall. Pat's face is a distorted mess of pain, his graying hair flies out in waves. He's still sweaty, the moisture ice-cold. Now both of his hands have gripped me during our shared ride down to the concrete parking lot. And somehow, the bastard manages to smile as we ruffle through the short shrubs.

I hear his head clunk. I feel his bones break and shift underneath my own. I black out. My head goes fuzzy. I see my brother at my mother's funeral, I see Diane crying over a woman she only met one time, and I see myself not crying at all until I'm in the (parking lot) bushes. I hear laughter and lover's whispers in the dark. I smell pancakes in the morning, see them on the skillet in the shape of a tiny heart. I hear (gurgling) (bubbling) (snarling) life and death. Diane.

My eyes open. It takes less than a second to snap back to reality. Pat is still beneath me, but he's almost not Pat anymore, and in a couple minutes, he's not going to be anything resembling Pat at all. If I don't get a move on, I'll see what the zombies do to him firsthand. His glazed eyes stare up at me. That same smile I thought I saw on the way down is on his face. He's no longer breathing, and if he were, he wouldn't be breathing much longer. His head split down the middle, brains leak out like pink stuffing in a Thanksgiving turkey.

The dead walk toward me with their arms out and their hands frozen into claws by rigor mortis. Rattles escape their throats. It's only a few of them at first, those close enough to hear the knock of bones on pavement, but their interests peak, and like any creature starving for food, they get excited. Their excitement alerts the others shuffling around the abandoned cars. There are no parking lot lights on. I don't know if this is a good thing or a bad thing, but I do know the faint moonlight casts eerie shadows over the zombie's faces, and that doesn't do much good in the way of bravery.

Still, I stand up. My lower back shoots with pain. I can't stand straight at first and there's a bruise already forming on my sternum, and when I take a deep breath, my lungs wheeze, causing me to double over with coughs. Blood covers my shirt whose blood it is, I'm not sure, but

I hope, and think, it's not mine. There are small green needles from the bush we landed on in my hair. An array of scratches from the branches on my arms and legs. A different yet equally terrible pain goes through my thigh. I look down to see a purple gash. It's shaped like I have to squint in the darkness to see it. A key? A key! I have since lost the keys to my car, and I parked way too far in an attempt to burn some extra calories.

How stupid. So seeing Pat's key is like a sign from God. I have to act fast. I look down to his smiling face. "You son of a bitch," I say. In the pocket of his gym shorts, a sliver of metal sticks out through ripped fabric. "Let's see what a big shot like you drives." I pull the key free, ripping the fabric wider and exposing his milky-white thighs which are covered in an even coat of black hair. The remote start has the Cadillac emblem emblazoned on it, silver on black. I see four buttons: lock, unlock, start, and panic. I scan the parking lot for the Cadillac.

The dead are coming in a thick wave. They're yellowish eyes glitter in the night. About seventy-five feet from where Pat and I landed is a two-door coupe. It's black and slick as hell. Must cost about sixty grand, but I guess that's what a job destroying the world will get you. I press the panic button. It takes a moment, and for a second, I think it's not going to work or maybe it's not his car after all. But the lights start flashing yellow and white. A horn cuts through the collective snarls of the zombies coming for me, and as they register the bright lights and terrible noise, they spin around and shuffle in the Cadillac's direction.

I let out the breath I was holding in, that sharp pain going through my chest and lungs. "Carly!" someone calls. I look up to see Abby's face floating above. "You're alive?" she asks. "Thank God!" I pat myself the way a cop might frisk a sketchy-looking suspect. "Yeah...I think I am." "Is Pat?" "No." "Oh, thank you, Lord. Thank you twice!" she says, but she's quickly cut off by Miss Seton's shriek. "Shut up!" she yells to the old woman, then turns back to me. "Yeah, we could use a little help." "Workin' on it," I say in a loud whisper.

"How are you up there?" "They're eating George. Some have broken from the pack and are heading toward the sound of the car," she shouts. "But they won't

stop coming from the hatch." "Stay as far away from them as you can. Go hide behind those air units. I'll think of something!" My head goes back to the parking lot. The dead have swarmed the car. They're clawing at the rolled up windows, banging the metal, snarling at an empty front seat. It's kind of funny, I think with a smile on my face, Pat probably double parked to give his sweet ride as much room away from other cars as possible and now zombies are junking it up. I pry my eyes away from them. There are three other cars on my side of the parking lot, none of which immediately offer me any help, and mine is the farthest away.

The clock ticks so I'll have to make use. One of the cars is a van, and I don't know what will be in the back, but I shuffle to it, feeling pain each time my feet hit concrete. There are no back windows, it's just a solid slab of black metal. I go around the front, trying both of the doors. Unsurprisingly, they're both locked. I'm going to have to break them, and sadly there's no way to break a window without it being loud. I pick up a piece of broken concrete, then take off my shirt.

The Cadillac's alarm continues to blare, but I think even the sound of shattering glass will trump it. I wrap the shirt around my hand holding the concrete. I hear a splat. A sickening sound, like a bag of wet laundry hitting the ground, landing on a sea of eggshells. I look up just in time to see a thin man with an arm half-hanging from his socket step off of the two-story roof. He seems to fall forever, his dangling arm fluttering like a streamer, then he lands in almost the exact same spot as whoever fell before him.

Another follows, this one an obese woman. She faces the chirping Cadillac, I can see the longing look on her face, pure curiosity over the sights and sounds of the car, wondering whether it's a potential meal or not. She hits and the spray of blood speckles the van's windshield. I turn my head back to the window. I cock my hand back with the shirt wrapped tight around my knuckles. I imagine Freddy's face where my reflection is, then Pat's. They're similar enough for me to barely notice the change, but I realize I'm slowly going crazy. At least I know I am now.

The glass shatters after two punches. I'm running mostly on rage and adrenaline, and I've only got a few seconds before my body starts screaming in pain from the fall I took. When I open the door, the inside light comes on. There's a steady dinging from the dashboard. An aroma of paint and stale body odor smacks me in the face. The first thing I see besides the brushes and cans in the back is a ladder. I've hit the jackpot. I climb inside to see how long the ladder is. It's not long enough to reach the roof, I'm sure, but if Abby and Miss Seton hang from the edge they'll be able to get their footing and climb down, a much better choice than the way I went.

I hit the unlock button and start to climb out of the cabin. As I do, my shoulder bumps the sun visor above the steering wheel, and something falls, cold against my skin before jingling on the van's floor. I look down at it, my eyes wide. This surprises me more than the ladder. It's a spare set of keys.

# Chapter Nineteen

I hold them in my hands. They're surprisingly cold on this hot, August night. Abby and Miss Seton are up on the roof, stranded, but the dead are falling off. Soon they'll be able to escape, or at least hold out until more help arrives. I can leave them right now, go get Diane, maybe even come back for them. Open your eyes, Glass, something inside me screams. They have the gun up there, at least I think. I don't know how many shots are left, but if worst come to worst and they can't hold the dead off, they can save two bullets for themselves.

I take a deep breath, now catching the faint odor of cigarettes in the van. The thought leaves a bad taste in my mouth. No, I'm not like that, I'm not Pat, I'm not Freddy. I am better than them. I hop out and run around back, pop open the back door. The ladder is one of those metal jobs that slides out as opposed to stands on two legs. I can do both, save them and Diane. I can. I promise I can. I'm not a Huber. Another zombie falls from the roof. I follow its descent and look down at the aftermath. There's a pile of squirming bodies not far from where Pat and I landed. Blood runs down the pavement to a sewer grate. A red river. I have to fight down a feeling of sickness in my stomach, then a twinge of pain in my lower back. The ladder is halfway out of the open van.

Pat's Cadillac still screams its shrill alarm, and I'm faintly aware of the other dead walking into the parking lot. Attracted and distracted by the noise but for how long? Another splat. Miss Seton screams on the roof, barely audible. I'll have to run the ladder a little ways down the building as far away from the pile and the Cadillac as I can manage without drawing more attention to myself. "Carly!" Abby screams. She sounds panicked. "Hold on, I'm coming" I begin to mutter under my breath, but something barrels into me, knocking my head against the edge of the van's roof.

A hissing noise fills my ears, like a leaking tank of propane. Idiot, I think to myself, you're such an idiot. You deserve to die. Warm, clammy hands touch my bare back. My heart shudders in my chest as I think a million different things at once: Why are these hands warm? Am I not the only alive man in this town? Has someone come to save us? I turn around, the hope in my heart blazing, but what I see quickly extinguishes all of it.

We had landed so hard on the ground, Pat's head split down the middle like one of Fred Flintstone's bowling balls. I had thought him to be double-dead, no chance at coming back like the rest of them. Besides, he said he'd avoided the virus, that some of us would be immune. Guess he was wrong. His eyes glow yellow. Blood pours down from his exposed brains like red syrup. I smell the decay on him. But I see that same flicker of life in his burning stare, the look of having one last meal. He leans on top of me, sending my head crashing into one of the ladder's legs. It hurts, but I hardly feel the pain. I flail my arms around like a drowning cat, then cross them over my face to prevent Pat from taking a chunk off of my nose. He snarls, but I kick forward.

The blow strikes him in the middle, sending his weight off of me. It gives me enough leeway to scrabble into the van. I can't close the door because of the ladder, but now I have the higher ground. The cabin light is on. The dashboard chimes, warning me I have multiple doors open. Pat is up now, his face a twisted mess of rage. He begins to crawl into the van. I grab the ladder and push with all my strength, which isn't much, I realize as the ladder smacks him in the face and drives him back a few feet. He grips the metal legs, letting out a growl that is so inhuman that it causes the hair on the back of my neck to stand up in hackles. "Shit," I say. I still have the van's keys in my pockets, so I hop into the driver's seat and pop the key into the ignition.

My strength may be nonexistent, but I doubt he'll be able to hold on to the van once I get it going. Another idea pops into my head, one of the killing two birds with one stone things except it's more like killing one dead dude with a van while I use the extra height of the vehicle to set the ladder on its roof thus getting Abby and Miss Seton out of harm's way. A peachy plan, indeed. The van purrs to life. I waste no time shifting the gear into drive. Its headlights automatically flip on, bringing the terrible details to life from the pile of splattered bodies a ways in front of me.

Abby is out from her hiding place on the roof, Miss Seton slumping next to her. She jumps up and down, waving her arms. In one hand is the unmistakable shape of the gun. She thinks I'm leaving them, abandoning them for the dead. To get under them, I cut the wheel to the right, heading for the front entrance. Our barricades have long since vanished, now looking more like the debris of a small, war-torn town. I see more zombies amble around the inside, dark shadows in the faintly lit recreation center. A man shuffling in the middle of the lot, unsure of which way to go, the blaring alarm of the Cadillac or the shiny new noise of the van turns his head to look at me barreling toward him. Half of his jaw hangs near his chest.

It seems to be only connected by a few strands of slimy, red strings. There's muck under his eyes, but no surprise in them as the headlights wash over his ruined clothes. The van flattens him. He goes under the wheels, causing everything in the van's back to jump; the metal ladder rattles, paint cans jingle. In the rearview, Pat still hangs on. The dead eyes staring at me. I slam on the brakes before crashing into the front doors. A dull thud hits right below the radio. Pat along with everything else inside the van lurches forward, but the dead, hungry look on his face never changes. I throw the gearshift into park but keep the car running. Before I get out, my eyes are caught by what slid up front. It's a hammer. The wood handle is worn, and the metal is rusty. I pick it up. It's not a gun by any means, but it'll do the trick.

Some of the dead have broken off from the Caddy, now intrigued by the sight of the van. A gunshot goes off as I climb out of the cab. My knees pop with pain. A thunderstorm of a migraine brews from the back of my head to my eyes. Concussion, maybe. A budding hemorrhage, perhaps. Miss Seton screams, and Abby's voice follows, but I can't make out what she says. "All right, Pat. Time to end this," I say. "I'm going to need that ladder." I round the van, seeing a twitching hand under the back tires. The man with the hanging mouth has a lot more to worry about than a dislocated jaw. Pat pushes off of the back of the van sluggishly.

He raises his arms out in front of him as if he's going to hug me instead of tear me apart. I waste no time. The hammer is old and used, but like I said, it does the trick. I hit him square in the top of the head, right where it had already split open and exposed red, goopy brains. I don't hit him with the head of the hammer. No, I hit him with the claw. The points squelch into the soft mess, sending sprays of scarlet mist into my eyes. I do my best to ignore this disgusting side-effect of re-murdering this asshole and nearly pull my arm out of its socket as I try to free up the hammer for another hit. But I don't need another hit. The yellow in his eyes goes a few shades paler, like the last embers of a dying fire.

He drops to his knees with the tool stuck in his head, fresh blood pouring over his face. His throat makes a wet click, and then he falls over on his side, twitching. I can't help the sick smile on my face. The gun goes off once more a thunder-crack over the blaring alarms. "Carly!" Abby screams. "Carly!" Despite falling two stories and almost dying, my body buzzes with adrenaline. I grip the end of the ladder and yank it free from the back, leaning it up against the van, then I climb up to the roof of it. A couple more of the dead have taken an interest in the noises coming from this side of the parking lot. "Abby, c'mon!" I shout and as I yell an attempt to broadcast my voice over the sound of the alarm the Cadillac shuts off. The dead and infected stop their snarls. I look to see them all turn their heads to the sound of my booming voice. Uh-oh. Then the gun explodes again, I see the flash from the muzzle, Abby's shaky arm holding it. A woman falls from the roof, splats about two feet from the hood of the van. Every last one of them (which has to be close to a hundred zombies) looks up at me. Shit, I think, if that lady landed on the engine, I'd be walking back to Diane. Gotta hurry up. Gotta save them and go. If I stand around looking like the world's biggest idiot, I'll have bigger problems than a broken car.

The metal of the roof whines as I pull the ladder up to my position. Black paint curls off, revealing bright silver streaks. I stand the ladder up. It doesn't reach all the way to the top of the building, but it's only short a couple feet. "Now!" I shout. The two women linger for a moment, then they kick into gear. Most of the herd on top of the roof turn their attention to Abby, but there are about fifteen feet of space between the nearest one and her, at least as far as I can see. "Hurry!" I shout.

Fifteen feet isn't much when it comes to a horde of the dead. I see her tuck the gun into her back pocket, and she goes from her knees to her stomach, then she sticks a foot out to find the first rung. The ladder won't stand on the metal on its own so I have to hold it, and as I stand here holding it, more dead swarm around the van. Their violent thrusts rock me. The ladder's bottom screeches against the metal, like nails on a chalkboard. They moan. They snarl. They reach out to me.

One taps the heel of my shoe, causing me to jump and the ladder to shake. "Hey, asshole!" Abby screams. "Hold it steady!" "I'm trying." She's halfway down when Miss Seton follows. I can hear her whimpers over the crowd of the dead. Her foot struggles to find purchase for a second, and I think she might fall. But she doesn't. "That's it!" I say. "Just like that, I got you!" Abby skips the last three steps and lands on the roof with a hollow thunk. She aims the pistol at a couple of the closest zombies and fires a quick succession of two or three shots, I'm not sure because the noise is so loud right next to me, my brains scramble.

I'm too focused on Miss Seton to really notice much of anything else. "Keep going!" I yell. Her whimpers turn into a fit of laughter, and the laughter bleeds back into a shriek. I see a pale hand reach out and grab at her salt-and-pepper hair. "No!" I scream. But it is too late. She totters, making the ladder whine even as I hold it, and I can't be up there holding her hands and down here holding the ladder at the same time. Miss Seton falls, hitching in mid-air for a split second as the dead man tries to hold on to his potential meal by a fistful of hair. I hear it rip cleanly from her scalp. It sounds like velcro. Her fall seems to last forever. During it, I swear she does the sign of the cross.

Her body splats on the concrete. A thin mist of blood escapes the bald patch on her head. She's not dead, the fall didn't kill her. I watch her squirm on the ground for a moment. Her leg is bent at an angle that it shouldn't be bent at. There's a glitter of white shards in a growing pool of blood around her mouth that can't be anything but teeth. But, damn it, she's alive. I lurch forward to try to save her, not thinking clearly. I'll do anything to keep her alive. Thank God for Abby. She grabs me by the arm with hands that feel like claws. "No," she says. "We have to go. It's too late." There are tears in her eyes, fresh tears.

The look tells me what happens to Miss Seton is not our fault, but I just can't accept that. I lunge again, her fingernails digging into me. "No! Let's go. We have a car, let's get the hell out of here." "How?" I shout, sweeping my arms over the crowd of the dead. They stare up at us with their hungry yellow eyes, some with fresh blood around their mouths and hands, moaning, groaning. She aims the gun at the windshield. As Miss Seton's screams ring the dinner bell. She yells for God. For Jesus to save her. These unanswered prayers amplify as the zombies tear her apart. I can't look.

A bullet hammers the glass, starring it. It's weak enough for me to stomp down, deftly avoiding a few dead hands. It buckles in the middle. I can't save Miss Seton because I have to save Diane. It's that simple. The windshield pops out enough for me to wiggle a couple of fingers in between and pry it up. Then it's completely clear and mostly still intact. I pick it up; it's heavy, but I'm running on straight adrenaline, I barely notice the straining in my lower back or the fresh cuts and pieces of glass embedded into my skin. "Go!" I yell. "Get the van moving." Abby freezes. "I-I can't," she says. I narrow my eyes at her. "Yes, you can. You have to. I'll fend them off as best as I can. They won't even get near you." Dead hands beat on the roof like dying fish on a boat. "You can do it!" I say. The look on her face turns into a snarl, then she plunges into the van's open windshield. I raise the fractured glass and swing it with all my might over her as she slides into the vehicle.

A couple of the dead take the hit straight in the face, mutilating any semblance of who they used to be. They're scalped, basically, and they fall like downed bowling pins. The next thing I grab is the ladder. I take out about five more with the ladder, though only momentarily. The gears of the van grind. The jerky movement almost throws me off, and I have to crouch just to keep my balance. Now I'm almost eye level with a man wearing the clothes of a priest. The white collar showing around his neck is dotted with blood. He's frumpy, too. And maybe a few hours ago, I would've recognized him as the one who'd helped lay my mother to rest, but now he's unrecognizable.

His bloody fingernails dig into the metal of the van like a can opener. I kick him square in the face, and he falls off. "Sorry," I say. "No hard feelings." The van bumps over a few of the dead, slowing us down. Abby steps on the gas. I lurch forward with the motion, still barely keeping my balance. "Go! Go!" I shout. And we do. The van's headlight, one must have broke as I parked it against the brick front of the building sweeps over a sea of shambling dead and infected citizens, and we head up the small hill toward the street and the town square beyond.

# Chapter Twenty

We break through the pack pretty easily. The van chugs along until we are on the dark road. Trees surround us on one side, the recreation center and the high school on the other side. When the last zombie is well behind us, I tap the roof three times and shout, "Stop!" over the whipping wind. Abby hears me and slows the van to a crawl. I come through the open windshield, not wanting to risk one of those things grabbing me from the woods, and I'm careful not to slice myself, although my hands are cut pretty deep and have since started to sting like I have a couple of bad paper cuts.

I grab my balled-up shirt, shake bits of glass free from the fabric, then put it on. Abby stares forward at the dark road. "You okay?" I ask her, and she doesn't answer immediately. I nudge her with my elbow. There's blood on her face. I don't think it's hers. She looks like she's been through hell and back, but so do I. "Yeah," she says. Her voice is small. "Now what?" "I save my fiancé," I answer. That's all that matters now. Not Pat, Not Ryan. Not Kevin, George, Earl, or Miss Seton. It's behind me, now.

We switch spots. I'm in the driver's seat. Abby looks at me, tears brimming in her eyes. A series of shuddering sobs shakes her entire body, practically the entire van. I've done it. There I go not caring about anyone else's feelings, as Diane has put it so bluntly. Abby has loved ones, too. We're in this together. Hesitantly, I stick my hand out to pat her on the back. I've never been good at this kind of thing, comforting people. It's awkward, and really, how can I make her feel comfortable in this mess? "Abby, what about you? Your mom and dad? I don't want to just leave" She cuts me off, her voice shaking. "There's nothing for me here.

My mom doesn't love me. Dad left" She looks up at me. "You know, I've only met him two times, and the last time I saw him he barely even talked to me. I was eight and his idea of fun was to take me to Home

Depot. Me, an eight-year-old girl to the freaking hardware store. Not to Build-A-Bear, not to get ice-cream, or anything fun like that. He gave me fifty cents and said, 'Go buy yourself some bubblegum, kid. I'll be by the power tools.' What kind of asshole does that?" I just shake my head even though I know exactly the type of asshole who would do it.

It's the type of father Prestonpans is so fond of, the Pat Hubers the Mr. Cages, the long-lost Ben Glass. I don't say this, there's no need. "I don't know," I say instead. Now's not the time to have a therapy session, not in the middle of the zombie apocalypse. "What about your mom? Was she sick? Do you think she...turned?" Abby closes her eyes, a tear rolls down her face. "When I left for work today she wasn't, but that doesn't mean anything. She smokes Cigarettes like a chimney, always looks pale and sounds like she's battling bronchitis.

I know she wanted to go to the festival, or at least watch the fireworks from the backyard." Abby snorts back a burst of laughter. "As if she doesn't see enough of those when she pops her Vicodin. So, Carly, her current state of health beats me. I'd bet money she's dead, just as I'd bet money your Diane is dead, too. Nothing personal, that's just the way it is." I don't know what to say, and I just stare at her with my mouth slightly open. My heart breaks slowly. I can feel every crack and fracture from its starting point to its end point.

That thought was always in the back of my mind. Hell, I saw enough death and chaos at the gym to realize Diane wouldn't have a chance on her own. But I'm not going to give up. I love her, damn it. I have to know. Abby swipes her eyes with the back of her hand. "I'm sorry, it's just" I shake my head. "Don't worry about it." "We have a gun. It's my dad's old hunting rifle,"she says. And these words are better than any apology. I won't be able to save Diane if I'm unarmed. If the motel is anything like the recreation center was, then, I'll need a rocket launcher, but a hunting rifle...well, it's better than nothing. "Where do you live?" "Tranent" Abby answers. Perfect. Right on the way to the square. I shift the van into gear, hearing the steady hum of the engine, its vibrations through the steering wheel, and I drive toward certain death.

It's a straight drive to the town's square once I turn down Redburn road maybe about half a mile away. The smartest choice would be for me to go the long way, but the van has started to cough when I drive over thirty miles per hour, and I don't think it'll last much longer. So straight shot it is. The street is lined with abandoned cars. They're parked off to the side, two tires on the road, two tires in the ditch. Nice cars, too. The festival brings a lot of out-of-towners in, people who are better off than the fast food and steel mill workers who inhabit Prestonpans. Maybe one of these cars would be a better option, maybe they would run long enough for me to get halfway across the country. Problem is their keys are probably in some dead person's cargo shorts, and we don't have time to search for them, nor do I want to. I'll keep the van for now.

Abby hasn't spoken in a few minutes, though I'll hear her shudder from time to time. A shadowy figure stumbles onto the road, moving like the ones at the gym. I slow the car to a crawl. Does this ever end? The shadowy figure pulls up on our right. It's a dead man, wearing a "Beat Prestonpans" shirt. There are claw marks across his chest, loose flesh dangling from his chin. "Even in death," I say, "North Berwick people are still assholes."

This makes Abby chuckle, then she double-takes. "Whoa, I think I know that guy," she says. My mouth turns to a thin line. "Where we are going, we're going to know a lot...of people."Except they're not people anymore, no matter how much they may look like it. Small flags are stuck in the grass on each side of the street, intermittently hidden between the cars. Their white, and blue colors sing in the night. I stop the van at the crest of the hill that leads directly into the heart of the town.

We stare at the chaos through the wide-open windshield. All of the businesses have their lights on: a Speedway gas station, McDonald's, a Mexican restaurant whose name I could never pronounce. There's a handful of fair vendors, too, with signs like: BEST DANG FUNNEL CAKES THIS SIDE OF THE Firth of Fourth, HOT FRIES!, FRESH-SQUEEZED LEMONADE! There's even a petting zoo in the middle of the street; the fence keeping in the small animals, goats, mules, pigs, llamas, and more, has long since been destroyed. Some of the animals lie in a pool of red, picked clean, nothing but furry husks of bone.

It's easy to see the crowd of people shambling about, the ones who've exhausted all sources of food but are too stupid to move with the rest of the herd that fell upon the recreation center. And believe me, there's a lot of stupid. This crowd makes the crowd at the gym look like professors. Some of them hunch over the last remnants of their meals, hands digging greedily into some faceless stranger or the remains of an animal. I can't help but think one of those people is Diane or my brother. The thought stings, causing me to almost pull over. I can't, though. I've come this far, have to keep going. "It's hell," Abby says. "Hell on earth."

I can't help but agree, not saying anything, but nodding. At the end of all of this chaos, shining like a beacon of hope is the Prestonpans Motel sign. Yeah, we'll really need Abby's gun. "Stop!" Abby says. "There, turn there." It's been so long since my high school bus went this route, I almost forgot where the turn to Abby's neighborhood was. The van barks and wheezes with the turn. "You wouldn't happen to have a better car?" "Better than this piece of shit?" Abby laughs. "It's sad, but no, we don't." We laugh together, the thin understanding that nice cars in Prestonpans are like a Leprechaun's pot o'gold at the end of a rainbow.

I turn down her street, and the smell that wafts through the windows of burning trash, and the factory pollution assures me that I've not taken a wrong turn. Welcome to Tranent Village. About two minutes later, I park the van in front of a metal box that dares call itself a trailer. It's covered in rust and overgrown lichen. A large tree stands to its left, branches hang out over it like suicidal people over a bridge. From a nearby nest on one of the branches, birds sit in a row of three, two of them unload white surprises on the trailer's facade.

It's so quiet I can hear the dinging of each one of their droppings like some sort of trailer park theme song. Abby doesn't notice this, and why should she? She's probably put up with it for many years. It's desensitization. But for me, this is a shock. Prestonpans is not, the prettiest of places, not rich, not a vacation spot, but I grew up on the other side of the tracks, again, not rich, but better than this. Compared to where I live in England, the trailer park is even more shocking.

I've forgotten what my hometown was truly like once you take off its cheap makeup and reveal its blemishes. "Stay here, keep the engine running. I'll get the gun," she says. "You gonna be okay?" She snorts. "I'm not a child." She gets out and bounds up to the trailer door. Like most places around this part of town, the door is locked. I hear her sharp knocks. No answer. She looks over her shoulder at me and shrugs. About a second later, she bends down and pulls a spare key free from beneath a welcome mat. The door creaks like the hinges are completely made of rust. Another faint smell of burning trash hits my nose. I look around the car, make sure there's nothing sneaking up on us. So far, there isn't. A shout causes me to bring my head up around, and I see a light flip on in the opposite side of the trailer, this side of town doesn't seem to have lost power yet. I see Abby's silhouette holding a rifle. But on the other end, I see another figure. This one is slumping, shambling along like one of the dead. Abby's mother, I think, giving me that terrible sinking feeling I've been hit with all day.

I jump out of the van, the gun with God knows how many shots left in my hand. I kick open the door like a police officer in one of the cop shows Diane is so fond of. The thin wood almost shatters beneath my running shoe. A burst of cigarette smoke and old, unwashed dishes pummel my nostrils. I am directly in the middle of them. One is a figure wearing a pink nightgown, graying hair in yellow rollers on her head, a face old and ruined from smoking pack after pack, backlit by the bright glow of a muted television.

The other is Abby who is holding her father's hunting rifle. Abby's mother turns to look at me, her yellowish eyes lighting up, a perpetual snarl on her face. She reaches her hands out, willing me to fall into her grip. I raise the gun. "No!" Abby shouts. "Don't. Leave her alone!" I can't. She's about five seconds away from grabbing hold of me. I slip out of the doorway, not watching where I'm going and fall over a chair in the kitchen. My weight carries me onto the kitchen table, flipping it over, causing an ashtray filled with butts and ash to cascade over my head.

Not smooth. Not Donny Zombie Slayer smooth at all. The gun skitters across the moldy linoleum. I faintly see it wedge under the refrigerator. "Do something," I wheeze as the woman gets closer. Rattles escape her open mouth. Black sludge drips from the sides of her lips, sludge that's probably been building up in her lungs for who knows how long. A hand closes around my ankles. I scrabble on the floor, knocking forks and plates everywhere. "Abby!" I scream. Her mother drops in front of me like a sack of bricks, teeth exposed, ready to clamp around the flesh of my calves. With my free leg, I kick at her, but she's not going anywhere. She's hungry, hungrier than all the others. I claw at her face. My fingers jam against the rough, wrinkled skin. Yellow fluid pulses from her nose, dribbles down her upper lip, threatening to coat me. I draw back. It's lost. Either die by disease or die by teeth. There is no, A gunshot cracks, all but blowing my eardrums to smithereens. Inside the small, tin box of the trailer, it's like someone set off a nuclear bomb.

My eyes reflexively shut. I scream, but I don't hear my own voice, only feel the sound grating the inside of my throat. Then it's all over. As fast as it started, it's over. When I open my eyes, I regret that decision. Abby's mom is splayed out on the checkered kitchen tile, what is left of her head resting on her bare, varicose-vein ridden arm. There's a growing pool of blood coming up to my body like a high tide. I'm too stunned to move. I hear Abby's sniffling. I turn to look at her, all my senses coming back to me in a roar. The gun smoke. The cigarette smoke. The death. Vibrant red. Dull yellows of the plastic kitchen chairs. My own heartbeat thrumming in my chest. The slightly jagged sound of Abby's mom's final death rattle.

Abby holds the gun at her shoulder. I see it waver and shake, catching the glint of the sterile white light overhead hit the barrel. "Abby?" I say, trying to get up, trying desperately harder not to slip in her mom's blood. She doesn't answer. I'm up now, making sure I'm not in the gun's line of sight. I reach a hand out. Heat blazes in the rifle's long muzzle. I push the barrel down so it points at the kitchen floor. Outside of the window, a figure passes lazily by. Another follows. I hear their moans as clearly as I heard them back at the recreation center.

"Abby...Abby, we have to go. We have to go now," I say. She seems to take no notice. I grab her by the arms, give her a slight shake. Her body is as stiff as one of the dead. Her eyes are wide open, staring endlessly at the thing that used to be her mother. A hand slaps the metal outside. We both jump as if it's a wake-up call. She looks at me, directly into my eyes, "What did I do?" she says. "What did I just do? I...I..." "You saved my life," I answer for her. "You had to do it, but right now we have to go. Is there a back door out of here?" Tears roll down her face as she nods. "Yeah, yeah, through the bedroom, but watch your step, there's a drop I shot my mom, holy shit, I shot my mom." "What do you mean watch my step? You're coming with me."

The growling outside grows louder. The gunshot drew them, damn it. There are only a few slivers of light between their dark shadows crowding the window. "I can't," she says. More slaps, these against the glass. "Yes, you can. You have to. What other choice do you have? Stay here and die?" "What other choice do I have out there?" she yells back at me. "I'll die out there, so will you! And your fiancé, she's probably already dead. Like my mom! Like my fucking mom!" The glass blows inward in a spray of shards. I grab her by the arm. She shrugs me off. "I'll come, but you have to give me a minute."

Her voice is oddly calm amidst all the chaos. Pale limbs push through the rest of the window, feeling around the wall with gnarled, arthritic-looking hands. The pool of blood has steadily taken over the entire small kitchen floor. A face shows itself through the thin veil of curtains. It's the face of a middle-aged man. He wears a trucker's cap on his head, a ratty, black goatee on his face stained with bits of gray and red. He's got the wild, infected look in his eyes. More of these eyes glow behind him and to each of his sides. "Just give me a minute," Abby repeats. But we both know we don't have a minute.

She bends down anyway. A hand reaches out to touch her mother's. "I'm so sorry," she says in a hoarse whisper. "I'm so sorry for never being there. I" The sound of busting hinges cuts her off. They haven't learned how to work a doorknob, but they know anything will budge with enough force. Abby raises her voice as if to shout over it, as if the louder she speaks the less likely any of this is happening. "I wasn't the best daughter. I never listened. I always complained. Broke the rules..." "Abby!" The door falls onto the small section of shag carpet with muffled grace, but the dead push in.

I grab the gun from Abby, but I don't fire it at the first one who's broken through. Instead, I raise the rifle up like a club and swing down on the man with the trucker cap. There's a loud crack as his skull caves in and brains ooze out. My back barks with pain. I gave the blow everything I had. There's no way I can do that again for twenty more. Plus, I need to conserve ammo to get to Diane. "Abby! Now!" I grip her fringed, recreation center employee shirt. "I love you, mom," she wheezes as I yank her up. A claw-like hand swings at her, missing by inches. The person who it belongs to, a girl with her blonde hair greased in blood falls down on Abby's mother with a wet splat. But her eyes never see the dead woman she landed on. No. They just focus on us.

We turn through a small doorway. Beads hang down from the frame, creating a distorted picture of Jesus. I plunge in. There's a small bed in one corner without a sheet, a nightstand next to it, an ashtray overflowing with cigarette butts sits atop a Bible. The door I see looks like a closet, but I feel the warmth from outside blowing through the cracks, and I open it. Abby is too lost to help me. She looks around the room with nostalgia-tinted lenses, realizing she is going to have to leave all of this behind.

The door opens up to a bald patch of dirt. There's another trailer across from us that looks almost exactly the same as Abby's except for the wreath on the door. Don't they know Christmas isn't for another five months? My guess is, yeah, they probably do, and if I went in there, a tree would be up in the corner of their tiny living room like it's been since 1985. Shadows shuffle around inside. Maybe I'll leave their Christmas alone. I have Abby's forearm in my left hand, the gun in the other. I'm dragging her around like a tired dog through the park. She's sniffling, not all here, but her legs still move.

That's all I can ask for. I press my shoulder to the side of the trailer. A puff of rust escapes the space between two metal sheets. Even in this heat, I can feel the coldness through my shirt. I peek around the corner. There are two ambling corpses not smart enough to follow the others inside. We shouldn't have a problem getting past them. I turn to Abby. "Hey," I whisper. "I need you right now, okay? I need you to be brave and smart." She looks at me with foggy eyes, like she's just woken up. She nods. "Abby," I say again, snapping my fingers. "I mean it. We are going to make a run for the van. But it's not safe, so if you are too slow and you stumble and fall, I might not be able to come back and save you." I sigh. "Abby, you did good, okay? You did what you should've done.

That wasn't your mother." As if me bringing up her dead mom is a kick to the head, Abby's eyes lose their glazed look. "I'll be okay, Carly. Let's go," she says. I look at her and nod, knowing she will be. Abby is strong, stronger than me. I give her the gun. We turn and run for the vehicle. I get my hand on the door handle right when I hear the crack of skulls. Two quick thumps, then two bodies hit the ground. Abby is in before me. Blood speckles her forehead and her face is red. I see her hands shaking as she sets the rifle between the two front seats. She gives me a nod, then says, "I knew them people. They used to babysit me when I was younger."

My lips part to say something comforting, but she doesn't let me. Besides, what could I say? "I didn't like them much. Always put me to bed before nine." I start the car, hit the gas, and get the hell out of the Trailer park.

# Chapter Twenty-one

The gunshot that killed Abby's mother did more than just attract a few of the dead. As I drive up the bumpy dirt road leading us onto the hill, I swerve back and forth like a drunk, trying to avoid the zombies. Their hands reach out to us, eyes lighting up as if the greatest meal they'll ever have is locked behind the metal walls of the van. The closer we get, the more there are. I hit one, hearing its pained snarls and coins jingling in the cup holder to my right as the body rolls under the back left tire. Another one throws itself at the front of the van. I'm not driving fast, either. Fifteen mph. There's no windshield to block us from the dead. So as I hit the bastard, I hope he doesn't roll up over the hood and end up being another passenger.

He doesn't. Instead, he's lost under the tires like his friend. The hill isn't as thick with the dead as the road which leads to the Tranent Village is. I turn right so I'm looking down the gradual decline and into the town square. If all things were normal, I'd be looking at a group of people laughing, dancing, and having a good time. But I'm not. What I am looking at is a graveyard, a wasteland. "Carly," Abby says. Her voice is weak and shaky. "Carly, look at that." "Yeah," I say. "So what?" She inhales deeply. This girl is younger than me by almost a decade and somehow she makes me feel like I'm a kid again who's getting yelled at for not doing their home-work.

Oh, Glass, what are we going to do with you? You won't get anywhere in life if you never do your schoolwork, blah, blah, blah. Still, she reminds me of a sister I never had. A sister younger or older would've always been there to be the level headed one. That much I always knew, especially when you grow up with Franky Glass as your older brother. Franky who would have said, "Hey, Carly! Go stick your head in that bulldog's mouth! What's the worst that could happen?" with a huge smile on his face.

Part of me hopes he is all right, while another part of me thinks it's perfectly normal for the world to seemingly end while he's back in town. What other way could it? "We aren't going to survive in that," Abby says. "Saving Diane is a suicide mission." She's right, but I'm willing to commit suicide. In the faint, red glow of the tail lights, a few zombies shamble toward the car. I'm not worried. They move about as fast as turtles. One of them is even crawling, their legs now broken and worthless.

We have time, time to figure this out. "Then we split up," I say. "Go our separate ways." Abby's features seem to melt off her face. She's a blank slate. Her lips settle to a thin line. "No," she says. "You didn't leave me back there, I'm not going to leave you." Her answer makes me feel a little better. I know I can't do this alone. I smile. "Then we fight our way to the motel." "I just wish I knew this wasn't for nothing. I wish I knew she was" She stops mid-sentence and turns her head to look out the broken windshield. Her mouth drops open. "What?" I say. "What?" this time a little more frantic. Her shaky hand raises to point ahead. I follow her index finger, and what I see fills my heart with hope. Just as the first corpse reaches the tail end of the van, thumping it with rage, I throw the gearshift into drive and roll down the hill.

The sign which reads PRESTONPANS MOTEL glows bright. It's meant to catch the eye of weary truckers who drive down the road with a deep longing for a bed and a hot shower. The next rest stop isn't for another couple hours down the motorway. There used to be one a few miles from Prestonpans, but it has long since been turned into a junkie shoot up gallery. The truckers who routinely pass the town on their way to wherever it is they are going know their best bet for a decent meal and a good night's sleep is the Prestonpans Motel...and, if I'm being totally honest here, their best bet for a midnight romp with Angie or Leah.

This sign meant to catch attention has been glowing steadily since Abby and I parked at the top of the hill, but now it flickers. Not just shoddy electricity flickering. No. This is all out, Morse code flickering. Someone is there and someone saw our headlights in the darkness, and now they're trying to catch our attention. My foot is on the brakes as we coast down the hill. I hit a roadblock going about twenty mph and turn it into splinters of plastic. Orange and, white dance off, of the hood of the car. Abby muffles a scream, shielding her face. Me, I just take it. Donny Zombie Slayer wouldn't flinch.

The smooth pavement of the road is no longer beneath us. Now, the tires roll over the downed, mutilated bodies of the festival-goers. Each rotation is met with a noise of boots stomping in mud, squelch, squelch, squelch,. But I hardly hear it. Blood sprays up in front and behind us. Any other time, I'd be vomiting out of the driver's side window, I'm sure. All I can think about is Diane. Her eyes glowing in the dark like a cat's. Her hair, so soft and always smelling of cherries, of life, not of the putrid stink of death all around us.

She has to be alive. Don't tell me I'm getting showered in zombie blood for nothing. Life can't be that unfair. I am in a daydream, dimly aware of Abby's shouts. To me, they sound like whispers. "CARLY!" The scream shatters my longing for Diane like a sledgehammer shatters glass. I turn to look at her and she's pointing again, but this time not at the sign. She's pointing at the parade float in front of us, two tires on the sidewalk, two tires on the road. I didn't even see it. Had I been paying attention to the best of my ability, I don't think I would've seen it anyway.

It's one of those terrible paper-maché jobs the high school art club throws together after classes are out for the day. I know this because it's a big, brown woodchuck with a football in its hand. Good ol' Prestonpans Woodchucks. I remember seeing the art nerds back when I was in high school, but let's be honest, I wasn't cool enough to hang with them. This float is sort of a tradition. I cut the wheel at the last moment, feeling the tires slip out from my control.

The road's too slick with blood and guts. The van is too beaten up. Abby's screams pierce my eardrums, somehow louder than the sound of the squealing tires. The van careens off of the road, jumps the curb with a loud thud followed by a pop that can't be anything but a blown tire. My hands are off the wheel now. I'm no longer in control. The car rolls. We are thrown around like rag dolls, only restrained by the loose seatbelts cutting across our chests and hips. I take to screaming, too, but I can't hear it over the sounds of crunching metal and chaos.

The airbag blows out of the steering wheel, punching me in the face harder than Freddy Huber has ever punched me. Blood spurts from my nose. It trickles down my lips and into my mouth, tasting faintly metallic. Then, all is quiet except for a warbled drone from the dashboard. The faint smell of fire reaches my nose. I feel like passing out, but the smell brings me back to attention.

I see an arm next to me. A stream of blood flows down it like rain down a window pane. "Oh," I say, "my head." My voice sounds so weak that I think I'm dead. Maybe I'm a ghost, maybe this is the afterlife. "Your head?" Abby says with a tang of sarcasm. "What about my head?" I look up, and there's a gash on Abby's forehead like a lightning bolt. Blood rolls from it, but doesn't drop down her cheeks. It falls upward where her hair is splayed out in suspended animation. That's when I realize what has happened. We landed on the van's roof. "You okay?" I ask, trying to sound manly, trying to sound in control, but knowing this is all my fault.

Her answer comes in the form of a clicking seatbelt, then the thud of her body hitting the ceiling of the van. She crunches a bit of glass with her elbows as she crawls forward through the windowless passenger door. "Well, okay then," I say under my breath. "Carly, hurry up!" Abby says. "They're coming." I already figured that, but I choose to keep my mouth shut. "The van's on fire," she finishes. "Well, fuck." My fingers start moving faster. Never in my life have they felt so much like sausages. Finally, I find the red button which releases me from this metal prison and drop to the ceiling. "Do you see the guns?" Abby yells. I stop, take a look over my shoulder and scan the interior as quick as I can. There's not much left of anything in the van.

Mostly just dented metal and ripped upholstery. It's like looking inside of a garbage disposal. "No!" I shout back. Her bloody arm reaches out to me and pulls me the rest of the way. We are in a parking lot. It takes me a moment to realize that, then a moment longer to realize what parking lot we're in, and then another moment to realize the army of the dead with their glowing, yellow eyes are practically licking their lips as they lumber toward us.

The lit sign to my right reads Eddy's Drug Mart, a family-owned drug store which is a lot like a more expensive Rite Aid. Greasy, black smoke billows up around the sign. It comes from the overturned van now spewing flames. Abby still has ahold of my arm as I get off of the pavement. There are no cars in the parking lot aside from the one I stole from the recreation center, but we did manage to knock over a small lemonade stand with a sign that reads: SUPPORT THE LOCAL GIRL SCOUTS BUY FRESH-SQUEEZED LEMONADE ONLY £0.75 A CUP! Sorry, Girl Scouts.

A few bodies are strewn to my left and right, their faces indistinguishable, nothing but a mess of chewed skin. I can't help but think how much they resemble Hamburger Helper. Abby grips me tighter and pulls. "Come on, through here!" And we are running. Well, she's running and I try to do something that mimics running, but my ribs are definitely broken and my head feels all woozy. She pulls me toward Eddy's front entrance, which is going to be locked, I just know it. If I recall correctly, Eddy was an old man last time I was in town, always complaining about 'those damn high school kids comin' in and stealing my chocolate and crisps!' If Everson is still alive then Eddy certainly is. There's no way he would've left it unlocked during the town's biggest celebration, either.

Abby pushes it, and whaddya know? It's locked. She doesn't let that slow her down. She picks up a rock from beneath a flower bed and cocks it back behind her head. The glass shatters on the first blow, sending large chunks to our feet. With her other hand, she pushes through the opening and clicks the lock. At first glance, you'd think Abby has done her fair share of breaking and entering. "The motel," I say, feeling not only pain in my ribs but also my heart as I slowly realize the chances of us surviving this dip to zero with each shambling, zombie step coming from up behind us. "I need to get to the motel."

She ignores me, and throws the door open. Above her, a bell chimes, signaling her entry. Something tells me Mr. Eddy won't be there to eye her suspiciously from behind his front counter. "Abby!" "Look behind you," she says. I do. The burning van has attracted what seems to be the whole fucking town. Skin hangs from their faces. Blood stains their clothes. They sway like drunks. Some of them have spotted Abby and me. They don't care for fire, they only care about the food. I will fight every last one of them to get to Diane.

I am so close, I can smell her cherry-scented hair. I see the Girl Scouts who were there to sell lemonade. Their faces are ashy, but for the most part clean. You might not think they were reanimated corpses if you didn't see their guts hanging from their stomachs, trailing out behind them like wedding gowns they'll never get to wear when they grow up. Beyond this group, there are more. Dare I say the whole county? They bump shoulder to shoulder, moaning and groaning, dripping with death and looking like a horror movie's worst nightmare, and that's saying something coming from a man who makes a living writing this crap.

Two of them are about three feet closer than I'm comfortable with. It's a man and woman, and something about the way they walk together tells me they were once married before all of this went down. So does the matching flag shirts. If they decided to walk a little faster and maybe lunge, they would have one large helping of Carly Glass for dinner this evening. I'm not offering, so I follow Abby into the drug store. "Help me," she says. "They'll break through the glass eventually, and I don't know how much time we are going to need. Once the fire burns out or the van explodes, they'll be knocking on the door." Inside, the store hasn't changed at all. There are rows of small shelves containing all sorts of bare essentials: toothpaste, toothbrushes, bread, peanut butter, soap, hairspray, brushes, milk and cold drinks on the far side. But closest to us, is a magazine rack full of Time, Life, Cosmopolitan, Us Weekly, those weird tabloid magazines, which today read: Is the President an Alien? Page 3! next to a picture of a man in a suit and tie with the face of some kind of blue reptile which is obviously fake.

Abby and I grab the magazine rack and slide it across the tile floor. It makes a ferocious squeaking sound that has me wanting to scrape out my eardrums with a fork and an even more ferocious burst of pain in my arms and ribs. Other than that, it works. "They'll push it over," Abby says, "if enough of them come this way. But it'll hold while we regroup." I nod, hoping she's right. I've been trapped enough today.

The couple bang on the door, rattling its hinges. The fire must be more entertaining because after a minute the banging stops, and I hear them scuffle away. "Let's get you bandaged up," I say. "You look like you've just been in a car...well, never mind. That was my fault. I didn't even see the float there." "I'm okay," Abby says, walking over to the aisle where the dishtowels are. She throws me one then starts wiping away the already drying blood from her forehead. "I think there's some peroxide right down there," I say, pointing. "Been a while since I've been in here." I look to the door which is almost completely covered by the magazine display, only offering a little slice of the parking lot and surrounding street.

Through that slice, the outside looks and sounds like the world is ending. "Not much has changed," Abby says. "Still think there's that Coke machine behind the counter, you know, the one that only costs a dime and gives you the glass bottles?" Abby shrugs, then turns back to the peroxide. "I'll go look," I say. The front counter is a relic of the 1950s. It's made of old wood and there's a window built in the front of it, showcasing a bunch of tobacco and cigarettes. The register is a dinosaur, one where you punch in the price of the item instead of scanning a barcode. It's both cool and unsettling to see. Sure enough, the Coke machine is there, also prehistoric. But man, I'm thirsty and nothing tastes better than a cold Coca-Cola when you're thirsty. As I walk around the counter, I say to Abby in a raised whisper, "I can't believe Diane is all right." "She might not be, Carly. Don't get your hopes up too much." Her words are like bullets to my heart. She's right. It might not even be Diane, might be some other survivors waiting for their guardian angels to show them the way to safety.

Abby must realize her bluntness because she says, "But if it is Diane, which it very well could be, then she's safe for the moment. It's us I'm worried about." I find a dime in the leave-a-penny-take-a-penny tray, then I put it in the Coke machine. The gears or whatever is inside the machine whir and an ice-cold, glass bottle of Coca-Cola fills my hand. I pop the top with the machine's built in bottle opener. "I'm sure there're a lot of people trapped, waiting for this thing to blow over," Abby continues. "And those are the ones who are smart enough to not try to take these things on." "Zombies," I say. "No need to be coy about it. George A. Romero hit it right on the head."

I'm looking at a display behind the counter. It's shrouded in darkness, the colors muted but unmistakably red, white, and blue. A cardboard Uncle Sam points at me with a speech bubble coming from his mouth. It says, "Uncle Sam wants you to celebrate the Fourth of July with Phantastic Phantom Phireworks!" "Whatever. The only problem," Abby says, "is that we aren't smart enough to just hole up until help arrives, and I'm okay with that. I don't want to end up like my mother. I want to get the hell out of this town.

We just need a distraction less dangerous than a burning van." "Distraction," I say, reaching out and grabbing a thick, red rocket. "I think I found our distraction." "Huh?" she says. She comes up the aisle to where I'm standing. "Fireworks," I say. I turn to her and see her looking at me with an arched eyebrow. For a moment, I feel like my older brother who was obsessed with fire and explosives like the rest of the kids we grew up with in our neighborhood. "Fireworks, really?" "It's not much, nothing like what the town has stored up for tonight, but it'll distract them enough for us to get a clear shot to the motel." This, I'm sure of.

"We need guns and knives, Carly! Weapons!" Abby shakes her head. "There's gotta be a way out the back, and I know there's an old ladder that goes up to the roof," I say, grabbing a few of the bottle rockets in one hand and a fistful of Roman Candles in the other. "Not the roof again. Carly, don't you ever learn?" "Grab me a lighter." She frowns. "Will you just trust me for once?" I say, a smile on my face.

# Chapter Twenty-two

Through the back door marked EMPLOYEES ONLY, is an array of shelves. On them, sits boxes of the stuff that is sold in the front. There is a small table and two chairs, an ashtray in the middle of it filled with old butts, and a deck of cards near one of the chairs. There is also a door. It is a looming metal door, with green paint that is now peeling and scratched in places, claw marks from a dog Mr. Eddy must've kept back here...or the thieving high school kids. In the door is a small window. The window is fogged over, but I see the brick building on the other side of it. The bricks belong to the family practitioner, Doc Hudson, who like his father before him and his father's father before him, is the Prestonpans town doctor.

I only know those bricks because every time my mom tried to bring me here for my routine checkup after one too many bad experiences with booster shots and finger pricks, I would break out of her grip and go running down the alley. In ten years, I really doubt much has changed, especially the ladder that runs up the side of Eddy's Drug Store. Nothing much ever changes in Prestonpans. Abby's shoes slap the floor behind me. I stop at the door, standing on my tiptoes to get a better view through the foggy glass. "Lighter," I say. Abby hands me a cheap, plastic Bic which I pocket. It's dark outside, but from what I see, there's no movement. The van fire must be a pretty good distraction...for this side of the town square, at least. "Wait," Abby says just as I grip the door handle. "What's the plan? I don't know the plan!" "Oh," I say, "I thought it was pretty self-explanatory." "Sorry, I'm not a smart ass like you. Just give me the gist." "If there's nothing out there, we try to sneak to the motel" "With no weapons," Abby says, a frown on her face. I pat the Roman Candles in my hand. She pinches the bridge of her nose, then stalks off back out to the front of the store.

A moment later, she comes back with two broom handles, their bristles detached. Unlike the late Ryan's broom handle, these aren't sharpened. "Here," she says. "It's not much, but it's better than fireworks." I narrow my eyes at her. "You ready?" "No," she says. I push the door open. The air is hot and stuffy. A typical July 4th weekend in Prestonpans, Scottish. A thick smell of garbage pummels my nostrils, but as I look to the metal cans to the right of the back door, I notice they're empty. The smell I smell is death, and it hangs all around us. I'll never get used to it. I can faintly hear their moans, their questioning, hungry moans, then the scuffle of dead feet over the pavement.

I try to not picture two of those feet belonging to Diane. I point to the left where the ladder is. Even in the faint glow of the moonlight, I can see the specks of orange rust on the metal. We walk. Abby stops abruptly, and it takes me a second to register why she has. A slow-moving horde passes by the entrance to the alleyway. Their faces are fixed on something, not looking toward us, but seeing them like that, so close, so determined, like a pack of wild animals roving the street for meat, almost stops my heart in my chest. I don't know I've walked backward until my heel bumps the trash can and the lid falls and clangs off the concrete.

It sounds like a truck smashing into a gong in the stillness of the night. I turn to try to steady it, to try to stop the vibrations, but that only makes it worse. The car accident has stripped me of what little grace and balance I had before and when I grab the can, I only knock it into the other and send it rolling down the alley. It could probably be heard in Indiana, it's that loud. Abby looks at me, her face drained of all color. "Shit," she says under her breath. The horde stops. In one motion, they all turn their infected gazes toward us. Their mouths are open, letting out deep groans, hungry groans. "Go! Go!" I say. The adrenaline coursing through my veins is not enough to vanquish the impending doom hanging over us. We can get to the ladder and climb it if we hustle. But my arms and legs are beaten maybe even broken and I'm not as fast as I used to be. We run, looking like two armies charging head to head in some great battle. "We aren't going to make it!" Abby shouts as the dead get closer and closer. I hear her footsteps stop then start retreating. I can't look back. I've crossed the point of no return, and just as I reach out to grip the flaky rung of the ladder, a dead hand snags my arm. It belongs to a woman of about forty eternally forty, now whose mouth hangs wide open.

Sludge pours from her moving lips. I rip my arm away from her grip, then acting on full instinct, kick out with my leg. A burst of white, hot pain ripples through my bones, but it sends the group stumbling back. I have enough room to climb up the ladder, and boy, do I climb fast. "Hey!" Abby shouts. She is trying to distract the group from me. I see her in the doorway of the drug store, one hand wrapped tightly around its handle. The horde couldn't care less about her. She's too far away. The real meal is right under their noses. "Stay put!" I shout. "I'll find a way." But really the only thing I think about is survival.

Flakes of orange, and black drift from the rungs with every hurried step. Most of the fireworks haven't fallen from my grip, cascading down to be stomped by the dead. I reach the top, breathing hard, then I take a look down to the alley. About thirty of the dead are grouped there, their hands up to the sky, gnarled fingers opening and closing as they hope for me to drop. Not going to happen. My feet have touched the surface of the roof now. For the moment, I am safe, but I am that much farther away from reuniting with Diane.

I turn around to look at where I'm at, to see if the roof has changed much since I was a scared eight-year-old who didn't want to get his shots. It hasn't besides the concrete boxes with their fans slowly whirring inside of them. I guess Eddy or his descendants finally sprung for some central heating and cooling. The roof seems to stretch for almost a full block, but I think I am just suffering from shock. The parapet comes up to the middle of my thighs. Not safe if I happen to pass out, but if I sit down with my back to the brick, I'll be okay. I just need to catch my breath, need to regroup. I crawl away from the ladder. The cool bricks chill my sweaty back through my shirt. I lost most of the fireworks. All I have left is a tube of Roman Candles, and the Bic Abby gave me.

There are not enough fireballs in it to take out thirty of the bastards, and there's no Army helicopter to signal. Fireworks? Yeah, a pretty useless plan, I guess. I look over the edge to where the motel's sign stands high in the dark about a football field and a sea of flesh-eating monsters away. It still glows, but no longer flickers. None of the rooms, have their lights on, not even the room Diane and I stayed in. This hurts to think about. Maybe she left. Maybe she's dead. I know she's afraid of the dark.

She wouldn't have the lights off with monsters everywhere. Then the rational part of my brain kicks in. Of course, I know she wouldn't keep the lights on. That would only bring more attention to her. I sigh and turn away, looking down the length of the roof. Something catches my eye. Something so weird that it forces me to stand up. It's two lawn chairs and they are angled toward the middle of the town square where the large cache of fireworks would've been set off to signify the end of the festival and another year of independence.

People were up here. Probably a dad and his son, or a boyfriend and girlfriend, only wanting to enjoy a show on a night off from the steel mill or the diner. This also hurts to think about because it could have easily been Diane and me. We might be zombies, but at least we would've been together. As I look more closely, my feet spur me forward on their own accord. A dark stain draws my eyes. I know what it is before I'm close enough to confirm it.

It's blood. Blood. Always blood. The whole town is drowning in blood. This blood is fresh and sticky. I limp toward it, saying in a soft whisper, barely heard over the rising moans of the dead, "Oh no oh no oh no." I see the hair first. Blonde hair, hair that looks just like...Diane's. Then a hand, a pale hand with her fingernails painted. They're an emerald green. I stop before I can see the face, my heart stopping with me. I don't want to see the face. I don't want to see my fiancé dead, her features twisted and distorted by disease. But I have to. I step forward, still far away, not knowing if I can get any closer. It's not Diane, but it's someone who I do recognize. A woman, who was once the most popular girl in high school, the same class as me. Prom queen, Homecoming queen, head of the student council. It's Bella Dawson, and ten years hasn't really changed her much, only her violent death has. Her throat has been ripped out, leaving a jagged, red smile in the skin.

Her eyes are no longer blue; now, they are rolled back, bloodshot whites. Blood stains her fingers and hands from when she probably tried to stop whatever did this to her. I never liked the girl, but it's sad to see her in this state. She was Freddy Huber's girlfriend. I don't know if they were still together, I know he still lives at home, he never got married, he's a momma's, A sound stops me dead in my tracks. It's a soft mushing sound. My heart leaps to my throat, now kick starting into overdrive. It's the sound of a feast. As the dead man looks up at me from behind the concrete box, his eyes blazing with yellow fire and his mouth dripping red, I nearly piss my pants. It's Freddy Huber.

It's like he recognizes me. The look he gives is of pure hatred. The others, like the ones from the recreation center and the ones currently trying to figure out how to climb the ladder that leads up here, always look hungry. But Freddy Huber must be full. He doesn't look much different than when I saw him yesterday. He's dressed a little nicer, wearing a pair of jeans and a button-up shirt now crusted with his old girlfriend's blood and guts, but his hair still stands up in that awful cowlick, and his face is still gaunt from the sickness that eventually turned him into a zombie For a second, I'm back in high school, back in the locker room after gym class. He's got me cornered in the last row of lockers, the row that has no exit at the back like the other rows, only an entrance. Now, it's not a locker, just two stories, a crowd of the dead, and the hard blacktop keeping me in the clutches of this demented asshole. He lumbers forward, groaning. Run! I tell myself. Run before your head is drowning in toilet water. Run before he bloodies your nose! "No," I say aloud. The sound of that word is like an angel's harp to my ears. "No, Huber. You're not winning this time." Without even thinking, I rip the lighter out of my pocket thank God it's still there, then I put the Roman Candle's wick between my thumb and forefinger.

The lighter strikes but doesn't catch. Huber is closer, bloody saliva dripping from his mouth like a rabid dog. A spark of flame shoots out from the Bic, but a strong wind follows it, blowing it out, and in turn, blowing Huber and the half-eaten Bella Dawson's stench full-force into my face. I flick the lighter again. This time, the wind doesn't blow. This time, the lighter sparks and catches. The wick sizzles, sending sprays of sparks in every direction. Freddy looks at it like a gullible man looks at a hypnotist's watch. Then the wick is gone, vanished into a puff of gray smoke. The smoke wafts into the air, and I feel the charging blast thrum through my fingers, the heat on my face. Just as Freddy snaps from hypnotized back to his primal, dead self, he opens his big, fat mouth. I aim the Roman Candle dead center. The first fireball shoots out at what seems like a hundred miles per hour. It's bright blue like a ball of electricity. First shot: Bulls-eye. Second shot: Bulls-eye. So is the third, the fourth. An array of colors burns inside of his mouth. Scarlet red, electric blue, dragon green, sunshine yellow.

His flesh smolders, melts right in front of me, dripping like candle wax. His eyeballs turn to pools of liquid inside of their sunken sockets. Fire burns through his cheeks, showing me teeth never properly cared for. He stumbles backward, moaning and groaning...but this time the sounds are different, this time they're pained, perhaps. I know it's just my imagination, but I think the real Freddy, the one that's not a zombie is still in there, and that Freddy is screaming.

I drop the Roman candle and it goes off a couple more times, sounding like thunder cracks. Freddy chokes on the fire, and I stand up as straight as my broken and beaten body will let me. "It's over," I say as I kick him square in the chest. "Fuck you." His arms flail out. The parapet catches him in the back of his knees, and he falls off the roof almost exactly like his father had fallen off the recreation center. But I don't go over with this Huber. The splat of his corpse is both mortifying and equally satisfying, better than any punch I could've thrown.

My own knees are weak, and I find myself collapsing. A choked sob escapes the back of my throat. Soon, the moans and shuffles from the horde below me start to fade. They are going to him. I have to see it. It takes almost all the strength I have left, but I grab the edge of the low wall and pull myself up.

The horde surrounds Freddy Huber. He is the flaming center of the dead circle for just a second. The bright fire is a distraction for a moment but not long enough. The horde splits up. They are back to their aimless lumbering, their unanswered grunts and moans of death. They head toward the alley, destroying my only means of escape. I look to the motel. Re-killing Freddy Huber was just a small victory, winning the battle, not the war. I still need to get to Diane, and I will by any means necessary. The pain in my body pulses, reminding me I won't be able to jump from roof to roof or swoop down from the heavens and save the day.

Above me, the white glow of the motel sign seems to dim. "Diane, I'm" A whine slices through the air, cutting me off. I snap my head to the direction of the sound or where I think it came from, it's so loud it sounds like it's coming from everywhere. When I see the bright streak of fire shoot from the alley, I know I've looked to the right spot. It pierces the night sky with streaks of red. Another follows soon after, exploding a beautiful blue. I hear Abby laughing down below. "Happy Fourth, you bitches!" she yells.

In one motion, despite the pain, I'm hunching over the parapet, looking over the edge, down to where she stands. The firework display hangs out of the door, and she rips the rockets off the rack and lights them like clockwork. Three more blast off into the air. The dead who were encroaching the alley are dumbfounded. All their heads turn to the fire in the sky. Most of the group starts to lumber away to the bright lights.

They move like a heard of drunken buffalo, but they move nonetheless. "Abby," I hiss. She barely hears me over the whistle, whine, and explosion of the fireworks. "Come down!" she says. "Fast!" Another rocket explodes to my left. The town square lights up like Vegas. "Diane," I mutter. With all the pain in my body, I force myself to grab the rusty metal of the ladder. I swing my legs over and step down as fast as I can. About fifteen seconds later, I'm on the concrete ground. The smell of fire is in the air. "They worked," Abby said. "You were right." "I told you," I say. She brings the flame to another wick, but I stop her before she lights it. "Wait, let me do this one." I grab the rocket with a hand that's covered in dry blood. It's a thick green one with PHANTASTIC printed on the side.

The alley is clear enough for me to walk almost to the end. I don't want to get too close, but I'm about three feet from the sidewalk, looking at the square, seeing all of its corners. Seeing, Freddy Huber, who's nothing but a charred piece of meat. Behind him is, the flower gardens with a red, white, and blue array of flowers in the windows. Next to that is Carlo's Diner, an antique shop called Relics of the Past. In the middle of the square are a few small trees, a fountain where dead, devoured people hang from the edge. There is a couple of benches. Dead bodies hang over those, too. I don't aim for any of these as I strike the lighter.

I aim for a telephone pole, it's a large, looming piece of wood, shaped like a capital T behind the Gardens. On each side of the wood are two rusty, gray transformers connected to a bunch of wires that branch off from it in a perfect square, and more wires which run the length of the town. The concept called Domino Effect flashes in my mind. The transformers are far but I know I can hit them with the rocket. Somehow, I just know. I light the wick. The sea of dead shift like calm waves, their heads tilted up to a flaming sky.

Abby must see what I mean to do. Her hand touches my shoulder right where the sleeve has ripped. Her skin is surprisingly cold and clammy. "Carly," she says. I'm picturing the town burning, picturing me putting an end to this place once and for all. "I have to," I say. The thought of Diane gone to the square to look for me crosses my mind, and of survivors hiding in these buildings, but I know that's not the case. Diane would stay put if she was okay, and I know there are no survivors in Prestonpans, especially not in the square. Everyone but Abby and I are gone. A, harsh, realization. The, truth.

The town is dead, and I have to bury it, I have to put the final nail in its coffin. The rocket explodes forward, its whistle muted by my own destructive thoughts. We are showered in an array of sparks from its back end. The zombies follow its line of flight with an almost human curiosity. The rocket hits the transformer in an explosion of purple light. Fire follows shortly after, Hellfire, I think to myself. A few wires disconnect, spraying sparks of blue and orange. One whips the flower shop, more snap the air like angry snakes. A lick of flame crawls down the rotten wood of the telephone pole until it splinters and collapses. Burning debris showers the garden center. Some of it breaks through the roof, and it doesn't take long for the patriotic flowers inside to crinkle and wilt under the resolve of the flames.

Everything blackens and turns to ash before my eyes. Glass breaks. Smoke pours out. All the while, the horde moves toward this chaos. Flames don't crawl this time; they sprint from building to building, jumping the gaps the way Olympic athletes jump hurdles. The diner is the next structure to catch. Then, the antique store. Then, the bank. A few of the dead go up in a blaze, running into the crowd. The rest is history.

# Chapter Twenty Three

With the town burning, the dead distracted, Abby and I run to the motel. There are still stragglers, but they are too enamored by the dancing flames consuming the square to pay us any attention. The motel is about half a block from the square. We hobble up Main Street, through the pools of blood. We tiptoe over the ruined bodies of people I faintly recognize, of people Abby whispers soft prayers to. It's like we are walking through a WWII battlefield. There're not many dead roaming or otherwise at the motel, not anymore. I can see room 111 where Diane and I stayed the past night with its curtains drawn. I pick up my pace as I round the corner of Main and break onto Second.

Abby grabs my shoulder and says, "Wait," in a whisper. A group of zombies lumbers out from behind a row of parked cars. A bunch of guys who were probably drunk before all this shit went down, maybe ten years older than me and dressed in the Prestonpans, Going-Out Attire, blue jeans, plaid shirts, trucker hats with their favorite beer company's logo embroidered on the front. Except, blood stains their clothes like it's this summer's hottest accessory. One of the guys' insides dangles from an open gash in his chest. A shiny fist-like organ. I swear it's the guy's heart. It bounces up and down like a large medallion. I want to kill them, too. Want to put them out of their misery, but we let them pass.

As I stare at them laboring on toward the flames that will no doubt turn them to piles of ash, I see the curtains part slightly from the corner of my eye. Someone looks out onto the street. My breath catches, heart drops like I'm at the top of a roller coaster's biggest hill and about to plunge down. "Dar " I almost shout, but Abby wraps her hand around my mouth, cutting my stupid burst of excitement off. One, of the dead stop, the one with his heart literally on his sleeve, and looks toward us with gold eyes.

A long moment passes before he turns back toward his comrades and starts walking again. "Sorry," I say shaking my head. "That was stupid." Once the group of dead is completely out of sight, I cross the parking lot and go to the door, my heart pounding in my chest. I knock once, softly. "Diane," I whisper. The door cracks. No light escapes the room. Instead, a flash of metal pokes out, and I stare down the barrel of a gun, looking into the black hole of the muzzle. Now the roller coaster I felt like I was on has derailed.

It was all for nothing. I didn't think my heart could break anymore than it already has. But it does. It can't be Diane because as far as I know, Diane does not have one of these. "Room's taken, buddy," a gruff voice says from under the cover of the shadows. The barrel of the gun pushes out farther. It's a Magnum, something Clint Eastwood would carry around with him in Dirty Harry. "Diane. I'm looking for Diane," I say, and I don't know how I speak. Maybe it's because this wouldn't be the first time I'm staring down the wrong end of a gun, maybe because I've seen the dead rise, maybe because I've done my fair share of killing both dead and alive and it's time for me to be judged. Or maybe I really am a changed man. I push the door open. Abby tries to grab at my shirt sleeve, but it's too late. She misses. The flames billowing up behind me paint the room as well as the man standing in front of me in a sickly, orange glow.

There are two packed suitcases on the bed Diane and I made love on no less than a day ago. The sheets are still half-splayed out on the shag carpet. A faint smell of cherry, Diane's shampoo is in the air. It takes me a moment to realize who the man is that stands in front of me, but it takes me almost no time at all to realize who the woman sitting in the chair on the far side with her knees drawn up to her chest is. It's Diane, and the man who is now lowering his Magnum in front of me is my older brother and at one point in my childhood, my arch nemesis, Franky.

My body begins to shake, the steady vibrations of a rocket about to explode. I shove past him. "Oh my God! I can't believe it," I say. Diane is in my arms in less than three seconds. I kiss her long and deep. Tears roll down her cheeks, dampening my face. Her body shudders with sobs. Happy sobs. "I knew you wouldn't let them get you. I knew it!" she says, almost blubbering. I hold her for just a moment longer. I never want to let her go, never again. "Shh!" Frank says. "Get in, get in!" "Why did you have to try out the gym? Why? Why?" Diane says.

She's bawling now, hitting me in the chest with her barely-clenched fists. It hurts, the physical toll of my journey catching up with me, but I don't care. She could shoot me, and I'd die happy. "I kept her safe for you, little sis," Frank says in a hushed whisper. He locks the deadbolt, then goes to look out the window. "Jesus, what did you guys do? Was that you shooting those freaks? Where's the gun? We need all the firepower we can get right now." "Fireworks," I say, never taking my eyes off of Diane. "Found some in Eddy's Drug Store.

Thought they'd be a distraction but wound up burning the whole town down." After a pause, I continue. "It needed to be burnt down." There's iron in my voice a confidence I've never heard before. Just like I'd imagined Donny Zombie Slayer to sound in my novel. Frank laughs, causing me to look at him. It's the laugh he used to use whenever he blamed something on me when we were kids. No one talks for a moment until Abby breaks the silence. "Hi, I'm Abby by the way," she says fom near the bed. Her shoulders slump and her eyelids sag, but she waves. I think she may fall onto the bed and sleep for a solid eight to ten hours. "I've heard a lot about you, Diane." Diane smiles. "I couldn't have done it without Abby," I say. "Nice to see you," Diane says, then turns back to me. "You should've never gone.

We should've never come here." The words come out of her mouth like lines from a script she's practiced constantly. "She's been saying that all night," Frank says. "Good thing you came along. I was this close from dragging her out of here once I saw the fire." I stand up, squaring up with my older brother. He's got a few inches on me, and a few more pounds, not to mention the Magnum, but I don't let that scare me. Abby and Diane look on like people who are about to witness something terrible.

I've described my older brother's brutality to Diane many times. She knows as well as I know how I've always wanted to punch him in the face, how I've always wanted to retaliate for what he did to our family by leaving so many years ago. But I don't hit him. I stick out my hand. He looks down at it like it's an alien limb. Maybe he was expecting a punch, too. After a moment, he smiles and takes it. We shake. I make sure it's a firm shake, one a military man could be proud of. "Wow," Frank says. "You've gotten a little stronger since you were thirteen." "Thank you, Frank," I say. "Thank you so much." He shrugs. "It was nothing. We are family after all, right?" "Right," I agree.

The handshake turns into a hug, one overdue by many years. Now it's my turn to cry. I've missed my older brother. Him protecting Diane, the love of my life, erases all he's ever done to hurt me. It only took forever, but Frank Glass has finally done right by me. He hands me the Magnum when we part. "You look like you can handle this better than I can." He looks me up and down, probably noting the blood and guts and dirt caked to my skin and clothes. "You've been on the battlefield. This mission needs an experienced soldier.

Think you can handle that?" I'm hesitant. This is like a passing of the torch. Older brother finally respects little sister. A, watershed moment. "I can handle it," I say. Frank smiles a genuine smile I've not seen on his face in a long, long time. "Good," he says, "because you're gonna lead us out of this fuckin hellhole town." I look over my shoulder with the cold iron in my hand. Abby and Diane have scooted closer together. They are so starkly different. Abby with her mess of brown hair and youthful face, the little sister I never had. Diane with her ringlets of blonde and those deep, emerald pools for her eyes.

The fear is no longer plastered on their faces. Diane nods to me, a faint smile on her lips. "How?" I say, turning back to Frank. "How do we get out of here?" The light from the fire cuts through the curtains. Smoke has been steadily drifting under the door, filling the room up with an acrid smell and a taste of destruction. The moans, and groans of the dead rise to double-dying shrieks of alarm. "I didn't park far," he says. "Had to leave the Jeep on the high Street because of the festival, but if they're all in the square like it sounds, we shouldn't have too much trouble getting there.

It won't be any trouble if you're leading us." "We shouldn't have any trouble as long as you don't let him drive," Abby says, smiling. Then she leans closer to Diane and whispers, "Don't ask," as if they've known each other all their lives. "Clock's running," Frank says. I exhale a deep breath, walk over to Diane, and kiss her more fiercely than I ever have. Then I am at the door, twisting the deadbolt. The group, Diane, Abby, and Frank line up behind me. Abby and Diane each carry a suitcase; Frank has his keys in hand.

I open the door. A wave of heat and smoke wash over us. The group of the dead who almost heard me shout for Diane earlier must not have liked the fire because they shamble back the way they came. It doesn't matter, though. The fire is bigger than it has ever been. The flower shop is nothing but ashes. Carlo's Diner will be next to nothing by the time we get to the car. Blackened bodies lie on the sidewalk, their hands outstretching in a last-ditch effort to claw away from the flames which consumed them.

They are indistinguishable save for the shapes of their jaws and the lengths of their bodies. The small patch of trees in the square has lost most of their leaves, letting us see that the fire has no intention of stopping. The night air glows a bloody red. "Over there!" Frank shouts, stifling a cough. I cut through the motel's parking lot. My eyes squint in an attempt to shield them from the smoke. Diane's right hand is latched to my elastic waistband, Abby to hers with Frank straggling behind.

We are almost a human chain. Stronger, together. The dead untouched by the flames see us through the haze of smoke, their eyes glinting yellow like gold coins in the sun, and speed up their ragged pace. I raise the Magnum and let loose three shots which are loud enough to topple over the rest of the town. One takes a bullet to the chest. It blows a hole about a foot in diameter in his middle. I can see the charred front of a building right through him. The other shots take off the tops of their heads. The one with his heart on his sleeve falls to his knees a few inches shorter than he was half a second ago, and slaps the sidewalk wetly. "That was Billy Frazer!" Frank shouts. I barely hear him over the roar of the flames and the ringing in my ears. "Not anymore!" I shout back.

My shooting arm vibrates with pain. The gun has a hell of a kick. When I see the flashing taillights of Frank's Jeep, I launch Diane and Abby forward. "Go! Get to the car, I'll cover you guys!" Another building falls in on itself, burying the three dead I just shot and giving me a clear view of the hill which Abby and I came down from. Beyond that is the top of the Prestonpans Recreation Center. I see the faint outlines of the flags whipping in the wind. I hope the fire doesn't stop until it reaches there, too. I hope the bodies of George, Earl, Miss Seton, Ryan, and even Pat are cremated, their ashes scattered in the wind. I hope they rest in peace.

Frank passes me, grabbing ahold of my sleeve as he goes by. I shrug him off. The chaos is almost picture-perfect. Something so beautiful, yet so sad. I can't stop looking at what I've done. "Come on!" Diane shouts. "I don't want to lose you again!" That snaps me out of it, and I head to the car. Frank is in the driver's seat, Abby in the front, Diane in the back, her door still open. The dark road ahead of us is empty except for a few straggling shadows on the horizon, undoubtedly more of the dead drawn out by the allure of bright flames. "Where are we going?"

Frank says. He turns the key in the ignition and the Jeep hums to life. "Anywhere but here," Abby says. "We'll go through North Berwick. It's where I live, then, we'll hit England. See if this thing has hit the whole country yet," he says. I barely hear them because I'm staring at the town square again, watching the flames dance and consume the buildings and the people I once knew.

Where I grew up is now gone. All that's left is a graveyard of bones, rotting flesh, and ashes. Diane tugs at my sleeve. "Come on," she says, a hint of panic in her voice. I crawl into the car, close the door, and she wraps her arms around me. As the Jeep lurches forward, I look out the back window and smile. What our futures hold, I don't know, but I do know I am with my family, and we have survived for now.

# The End

# Also by michael paterson

Bombing Belfast
Nikki's Nightmare, Zombie Invasion
Victim's of The IRA
The Runaway
Beast from the Fog
VIXEN
My Wife the Assassin
Jacks Destiny
Life's Entirety
Happy Ending
Children Unknown
Ben and the Magic Crystal
Abducted and Unknown
Ian the Ice Cream Man
A Cruel World
Coming Out; Every Love Deserves Respect
Her Saviour
My New Life
Nikki's Nightmare, Zombie Invasion
Eden the Day Her World Changed
Carly the Zombie Slayer

Lightning Source UK Ltd.
Milton Keynes UK
UKHW010932060223
416537UK00002B/581